For those who take

the path less taken.

Prologue

Tabitha

I trail in the wake behind my brother and his new girlfriend, the three of us paddling in kayaks across the surface of Lake Walton, slicing our oars through the dark water at a leisurely pace.

The day is calm, sunny, and perfect.

I adjust the brim of my straw sunhat so it completely covers my face, and push the sunglasses up higher on the bridge of my nose before maneuvering my kayak closer to my brother, Cal, and his girlfriend, Greyson.

They're ahead of me, rowing side by side in companionable silence, and I trail after them, in no hurry to partake in their love-fest.

I try to avert my eyes when they steal glances at each other every couple feet as they paddle, trying to be sly about it but failing miserably. They cannot keep their eyes off each other, and if I weren't so damn happy for my brother, I would be completely repulsed.

Nonetheless, as a single female, I feel it's my duty to give an eye-roll towards the cloudless blue sky.

"Babe, let's check out that sand bar over there." My brother's low voice carries back to me. He twists his lean torso and looks back at me. "Tab, we're gonna stop at the island."

"Hey, I know that place!" Greyson exclaims, excited. "You showed me a picture of it once."

Cal grins at her, obviously pleased that she remembered, and we all paddle deftly towards the little island. It's actually more of a peninsula jutting out into the water, with a white sand beach, picnic tables, and a campfire site.

As we get closer, I can see a small smokestack where the last campers had their bonfire, the faint, smoldering gray cloud rising into the canopy of trees from the dying embers.

My brother continues talking. "I've always wanted to stop, but stopping by myself always just seemed depressing."

Greyson blushes at him prettily. "Well, now you never have to."

My brother's steely gaze lands on the cleavage appearing from beneath the zipper of her life jacket. "Kayaking with you is almost worse."

Her large hazel eyes widen. "What! Why?"

"Because I just keep wanting to lean over and pull you into the water. Get us both wet."

Gross. I want to splash them both with my paddle. "Alright, you two, stop. Just stop. You're making me sick."

My brother, who I never in a million years thought would so freely give PDA, leans his muscular, tattooed arm out to draw Greyson's kayak closer, and he bends over the side of his, puckering his lips.

Their eyes close behind their sunglasses and their lips meet, pressing together over the water.

They both sigh.

Greyson lays her paddle across her red kayak, the delicate fingers of one hand reaching up to gently stroke the new gash under my brother's left eye. "I have to put some Neosporin on this." Her voice drifts over the water, soothing. "I'm worried."

My annoying younger brother nods into her palm like a puppy dog. "Okay."

What the…

Seriously, could this get any worse?

"I brought us a picnic."

Never mind. It just did.

Greyson gasps in delight. "Oh my god, Cal, sweetie —could you be any more perfect?"

"I don't know. Could you?"

"I love you."

"I love *you*."

They're disgusting. Just disgusting.

Greyson sighs.

I sigh too, and with a jealous little huff, keep paddling.

Our kayaks hit the sandy bank of the island, and Cal hops out first, dragging Greyson's up onto the shore with ease, and holding his hand out to steady her while she steps out onto the beach.

I hold back a groan when his hands go around her waist and their lips meet for another quick kiss. He gives her butt a swat when she starts up the bank towards the campsite.

My brother turns, wading in a few feet, and grabs the rope at the front of mine, pulling my kayak alongside Greyson's and extending his hand to me the same way he did for her. Only instead of graciously accepting his help, I narrow my eyes at him from my spot on the water.

"What's the look for?" he asks, glaring down at me.

"I don't trust you," I say.

Cal snorts. "What—you think I'm going to dump you in the water? What are we, thirteen?"

"Oh *please*. I know how you operate. Don't tell me you aren't thinking about it right now," I tease, but extend my hand.

He takes it, pulling me up so I can step out. When my feet are on the shore, I'm ankle deep in water and my brother crosses his arms indignantly.

"You give me no credit at all. I would never shove you in the water."

Now I'm laughing as I stand. "You are such a liar."

"What kind of an asshole shoves his sister in the water with his girlfriend watching?" He leans over as he bends to steady my kayak, busying himself by pulling them onto the shore farther so they don't float away. "You know—" he looks slyly over at me "—you're right. I did think about shoving your ass in the water."

"I knew it!" My foot gives a kick, and I splash him.

"Yeah, well, you deserve it. I still owe you from the time you laid under my bed hiding while I changed my clothes, then scared the shit out of me once I turned off the lights and climbed into bed."

I throw my hands up, exasperated. "That was three years ago!"

"Whatever—you're sick. Watch your back, that's all I'm saying."

"Shut up," I scoff, glancing up to where Greyson is walking around the picnic area, alone, while we bicker like children. "And why are you bothering me when your girlfriend is waiting? I love you to death, but the two of you make me sick."

And I already love *her* to death—like a sister.

I love them both.

They have formed an unbreakable bond, an incredible friendship.

And I want them to continue being happy.

Collin

"I don't understand why you're not getting this one. It's perfect!" My sister nags beside me, pulling the lavender shower curtain off the hook and tossing it in the cart. "I think it's so cute."

I reach into the cart and snatch it up, replacing it on the display. "I'm not putting this in my new condo. It's purple. And floral."

My little sister *tsks*. "More like a grayish lavender. Girls will love this."

"Greyson, I don't plan on parading a string of girls through my condo, and I am not going to look at this ugly-ass shower curtain every damn morning before work."

She sighs loudly, relenting. "Fine, have it your way. I'm just trying to make your place a babe magnet."

I laugh and grab hold of the cart. "Let's just grab towels and everything else on the list, and then we can come back to this aisle. Right now, I'm over picking out shower curtains. Agreed?"

Greyson nods, her pale blonde ponytail swinging jauntily and settling on her shoulders. With tan skin from perpetually being out in the sun, pert nose, and large hazel eyes, my younger sister by five years is beautiful—inside and out.

Not to mention *kind*, sweet, and funny.

We are nothing alike.

Where she is all sunshine and light, I am stormy and dark. Greyson is five-foot-five and delicate; I am six-foot-two and imposing.

Unyielding.

I stand brooding beside her, leaning my elbows against the handle of the red cart as we trail aimlessly through the center aisle of her favorite supermarket chain. She lets me push the cart of household items and cleaning supplies I'll need for my new condo, chatting next to me about her new boyfriend, Cal.

We arrive at the lighting department, and Greyson halts the cart, nudging me. "Didn't you say you needed a lamp for your living room?"

I shrug, pausing to adjust the sunglasses perched on top of my head. "Yeah, but I was planning on just stealing one of Mom's."

Greyson tips her head back and laughs. "And you don't think she'll notice?"

I shrug again. "Maybe. But by the time she notices her lamp missing, I'll be long gone. It's a solid plan."

"But she'll see it at your housewarming party next

weekend." My sister knocks me with her hip. "Just go pick out a lamp, tightwad, and spare us all the drama."

"Fine," I grumble. "But explain to me why I have to pay thirty bucks for a lamp, then another twenty for the shade? That's highway robbery. All I *really* need is a light bulb and a switch."

But I comply, knowing it's a losing argument. She's going to make me buy a lamp no matter how long we stand here disagreeing. Striding with purpose down the lighting aisle, I eyeball them all and reach impulsively for a silver base with sleek lines.

There. This will do.

Now for a shade to coordinate; something simple with clean lines would work.

Sleek. Clean lines.

What the hell is wrong with me? *I sound like a goddamn interior decorator.*

"That one's actually really nice!" Grey exclaims excitedly, helping me rearrange the shopping cart contents to make room for the lamp and shade among all my other crap.

"Gee, don't sound so surprised," I deadpan. "I'm not a total Neanderthal."

"Well, I mean… not *totally*. Although your usual decoration of choice is Star Wars posters and The Incredible Hulk."

I scoff loudly, crossing my muscular arms over my broad chest resentfully. The navy-blue tee shirt I shrunk doing my own laundry strains across my shoulders. "I'll have you know, my condo in Seattle had none of those things, smartass."

"I'm only teasing… Mom packed all that away when

you moved after college. But I'm sure the boxes are in the basement somewhere if you're interested."

"I'm not," I insist with a scowl.

Well. Maybe I am, a little. But only because I don't have any artwork to hang on my white condo walls.

Dammit. There I go again, sounding like a goddamn decorator.

"Can we just grab what I need and get the hell out of here?"

"Yeah, yeah, yeah, hold your horses." Greyson holds up the handwritten list I brought, consulting it like it's a treasure map. "We still have to grab you a rug for your kitchen, and some gadgets. You need a wine bottle opener —" She's skeptical. "Really? A wine bottle opener? That's necessary?"

"I like wine sometimes. I need a new bottle opener." If sighing sarcastically were a thing, I would do it right now. But since it's not, I just do it loudly.

My sister relents, holding her hands up, one still clutching the list. "Okay, okay, calm down." She checks the list again. "*Wine* bottle opener," the brat emphasizes with an eye-roll. "Can opener. Water glasses. Garbage bags."

Greyson's voice fades out as I stare absentmindedly up the center aisle, the repetitive elevator music from Target's sound system lulling me into a zombie-like state. A leggy blonde up ahead wearing a hot-pink baseball hat peaks my curiosity—long, tan legs in white shorts and a light gray shirt. I perk up considerably at the sight of her.

She stops in the middle of the aisle and gapes, arms laden with shampoo and hairspray and shit, and the pink lips I'm admiring part in a surprised *O*. I can see from here that her eyes are bright blue, set off by the color of her cap. Without hesitating, I scan that body from the long blonde hair falling loosely under her hat, to the round breasts beneath her simple shirt, up to the shocked expression on her face.

No. That's not right—she looks spooked.

Like she's seen a ghost.

When she darts quickly behind a display up ahead, abandoning her cart, I crane my neck, hoping to catch another glimpse.

Fail.

Dammit, where the hell did she go?

"Are you even listening to me?" my sister asks, threading her arm through mine to recapture my attention. Knowing me like she does, she takes pity on me. "Tell you what. Let's quickly run over to the cleaning supplies, grab some detergent, and call it a day. Then we can grab lunch. Your treat, of course."

Her head hits my shoulder, and she gives my arm an affectionate, sisterly squeeze.

"Of course."

Tabitha

I put a trembling hand to my chest to calm this racing heart inside me. It's going positively wild, and I place my other hand on the shopping cart for support. Somewhere in the next aisle over, I hear the tinkling laugh—one that I recognize. One that I'm all too familiar with, and I know it's her.

Greyson Keller.

My brother's girlfriend…

…grasping the arm of a guy I don't recognize, pulling him towards a display of bed spreads, holding his tan, muscular arm firmly with one hand, and pointing to a quilt display with the other.

"You said you *just* wanted to quickly grab some more cleaning supplies," I hear his deep voice grumble.

"I know what I said. But since we're near the bedding, wouldn't it be nice to roll around on crisp, clean sheets?"

The guy's hesitation is followed by more grumbling. "I *guess* so…"

This is not happening right now.

I am not witnessing Cal's girlfriend cheating on him with another guy. I can't be.

I refuse to believe it. Squeezing my blue eyes shut, I lean my limp body against the metal rack of pillows behind me, and I use the rack to support myself. My legs are weak, wobbly, and I lower my palms to steady my knees, taking a few deep breaths.

I'm physically shaking.

I am *not* seeing this. *I'm not, I'm not, I'm not.*

I can't be.

Cal loves her. I love her, too—she's the sister I never had.

I can't even conjure up any nasty or unkind thoughts about her right now, even with the truth before me. One aisle over. The truth that's *laughing* and simpering and giggling like a flirty teenager. I love Greyson so much that I don't have the heart to storm over and confront her for being a lying, cheating, backstabbing…

Ugh.

I stare up at the ceiling of the store at the fluorescent bulbs now blinding my eyes, and I pull the brim of my hot-pink hat down to shield my eyes, debating my options.

I can't even think about her being a cheater.

Horrible.

I think I'm going to retch all over the floor in this aisle.

Oh sweet baby Jesus.

I inhale and exhale slowly, trying to catch my breath—the way I did in college after I'd had too much to drink and was trying to stop myself from barfing. I stand like this until my queasy stomach subsides, and the pukey feeling passes.

My lids flutter open.

What do I do? *What the hell do I do?* This is my brother's girlfriend, the center of his whole world, the love of his life. I cannot tell him she's cheating on him. I cannot tell him what I just saw—but at the same time, I can't unsee it.

I also can't stand here all day, hiding behind the bean bag chairs and pillows with a cart full of unpaid toiletries, as Greyson and *that hot guy* idly stroll, aisle after aisle, laughing and flirting and touching each other with familiarity.

There goes his laugh again. Deep and rich and amused.

Happy.

I thought *Greyson* was happy—happy with Cal.

Shit.

And suddenly, here they are. A million uncharitable thoughts race through my brain as I hide, concealed from their view. How dare she? How long has this been going on? How can she so brazenly flaunt this guy in public, where anyone could bump into them? *What do I tell my brother?*

My brother, who has never been in love until now. My brother, who has never let anyone into his heart. He will be *crushed*. Devastated won't even begin to cover it.

Cal will never trust anyone again.

My chest tightening and heart breaking, I take another deep, stabilizing breath and try to recall some of the breathing techniques I learned in yoga class. And... I got nothin'.

Crap.

Why don't I ever pay attention in that dumb class? *In through the nose, out through the mouth... in through the nose, out through the mouth.*

I peek my head around the corner to catch a glimpse of them.

Greyson and that dark-haired hottie.

Shit, he's deliciously attractive.

He's tall and broad with thick, dark brown hair and sexy black sunglasses propped on top of his head. Greyson has her blonde head resting against his wide shoulder. A large hand slides around my brother's girlfriend's waist, giving her an affectionate squeeze.

I hate it. I hate how comfortable they obviously are with each other.

How the hell can my brother compete with a guy as handsome as *that?*

I glare at them, sick to my stomach and wanting to vom, then plaster myself back up against the shelf with a shaking breath. A sharp price tag stabs me in the back, jolting me out of my angry stupor.

Why the hell am I the one hiding? I'm not the one doing anything wrong!

Another rich laugh fills the air, coming from the next aisle over, and I steady myself. Straighten my spine. Count down from three.

Two.

One.

I step out into the main aisle, plastering on a wide smile when I come face to face with Greyson and this homewrecking asshole.

"Greyson! Hi!" My voice comes out saccharine sweet, sounding hollow, fake, and robotic as I try my best to act surprised to see them. Surprised but cheerful. Definitely cheerful.

Gag.

"Oh my gosh! Tabitha!" Greyson gasps, delighted, and steps out from behind the cart, coming around it to embrace me. "It's so good to see you!"

Hmm, she sounds suspiciously joyful. *For a lying, backstabbing cheater*.

"Hey." My body is stiff, arms clutching the toiletries that haven't yet made it into my cart. I glance between the two of them bitterly from under the brim of my cap. "What are you doing in town? So far from school?"

She and my brother are in college three hours away, but coincidentally, our parents only live twenty minutes apart from each other.

Imagine that.

Greyson's painfully attractive date's eyes linger on me with rapt interest, his hazel irises checking me out from head to toe, landing on my chest a heartbeat too long, his high cheekbones taking on a rosy glow before jerking his gaze away.

Of all the nerve!

What. An. *Asshole*.

"We're getting odds and ends for his condo," Greyson replies slowly, stepping out of our embrace and narrowing her eyes as she studies me. My brother's girlfriend might be stupidly gorgeous, but she's definitely not stupid. "Tabitha, what's wrong?"

"Nothing," I lie, shaking out of her grasp. "Who's your *friend*?" Agitated, I begin tapping my foot on the hard tile, biting my tongue.

Greyson's lip's part, and I brace myself for her lie.

"You mean Collin?" Confused, she looks back and forth between him and me, apprehension marring her beautiful face. "Tabitha, I'm not sure—"

"How *could* you?" I hiss in a whisper.

Her expressive eyes get wide. "How could I what?"

"Oh my god, seriously?" I raise my palms in frustration, the deodorant, hairspray, and toothpaste falling to the ground with noisy, hollow clangs. The metal hairspray can bounces, rolls, and hits the adjacent metal shelf, but I don't even care.

"How could you *do* this to my brother? He loves you!" It takes every ounce of my self-control not to have an outburst, but based on the shrill sound coming out of my mouth, I'm not successful.

"Tabitha, tell me what's wrong, *please*. You're scaring me," Greyson implores, reaching for my arm.

I jerk it away.

Upset and near hysterics, I turn to leave, bending with a sob to snatch my purchases off the ground. "Whatever you're going to say, save it, okay? Enjoy your *ridiculously* good-looking boy toy. I'll be there to pick up my brother's broken pieces after you break his heart into a million little shards."

I turn to stalk away.

"What!" Greyson gasps from behind me. "Oh my god—"

"Hey!" the dark-haired Adonis bellows after me, taking several long strides and cuffing his large, warm hand over my bicep. "Get your bony ass back here for a second."

Bony ass? *Bony*. Ass?

"H-how dare you!" I sputter furiously; whether it's from the manhandling or name calling, I'm not entirely sure.

"How dare *I*? You're the one that sounds like a mental person. That's my *sister*. Greyson is my sister."

Okay.

Yeah.

So this is the part where I stand there dumbfounded, staring at both of them with my mouth agape. Yup, that's what I do. I stand there, gaping. Embarrassed. Face flushed. Horrified. Mortified.

As far as misunderstandings go, this is one of the worst.

"I... oh."

"Yeah, *oh*. What the hell is wrong with you?"

"I didn't... I didn't think."

"You didn't think? I can see that." He runs a tan hand through his dark, mussy hair. "Nice to meet you, by the way. I'm Collin Keller. Greyson's *brother*."

Collin Keller extends his hand, and I gawk dumbly at it, still sheepish. He leaves it there, hanging between us, waiting for me to shake it.

"I... Hi." My hand slides into his and I shiver. Our eyes connect.

They're hazel.

His eyes are hazel, just like Greyson's.

Exactly. Like. Greyson's.

As we take each other in, the hard set of his mouth transforms; the corners of his beautifully sculpted lips tip into an awkward smile, framed by the shadow of a beard playing along his strong jawline and defined chin.

He's *so*... male.

"You don't have any pictures of him on Facebook," I blurt out, releasing Collin's hand and wiping any traces of him off on my white shorts.

He studies me then, awareness prickling the back of my neck. We regard each other intently before he turns towards his sister, his eyebrows going up quizzically.

"You don't have any pictures of me on Facebook? Why the hell not?"

She laughs and smacks him in the arm. "You said you *hate* when I tag you in pictures. Besides, you haven't even been in town the last two years. So I have almost no recent pictures of you. Unless you count the ones where our whole family's wearing matching Christmas pajamas."

He chuckles then, deep and low and manly. God, his voice is sexy. His hazel eyes shine and my breath hitches for the second time today. "Fair enough." He regards me then with another grin. "She's right, I *do* hate when she tags me in pictures."

I shake my head, miserable. "I'm sorry, Grey. I can't believe I thought…"

She nods, understanding. "I know what you thought, and I don't blame you."

I'd feel so much better if she called me an asshole. Or an overreacting jackass.

I deserve it.

"Yeah, it's just. When I saw you touching him…" I let my judgment trail off suggestively, glancing back and forth between the two of them with raised eyebrows to emphasize my point. "You and him, my imagination ran a little wild."

If only she knew how wild my imagination really was.

"Ya think?" Collin deadpans beside her.

Greyson ignores him, shaking her head before reaching over, pulling me in for a hug. "Collin just accepted a job offer," she murmurs into my hair. "He just moved back to the city from Seattle. I'm helping him buy a bunch of stuff for his new condo."

All I can muster is a weak, "Oh," when she pulls

away. Then meekly, I say, "In my defense, except for the eyes, you two look nothing alike."

"Thank *God*," Collin jokes, and Greyson playfully smacks him again.

"Hey!"

"Sorry, but you're the least attractive of mom's three children."

Greyson rolls her large hazel eyes. "Anyway, I feel horrible you thought that me and him... I mean. Look at him—*so* not my type."

Oh, I'm looking alright. As if I could stop myself.

I fidget with the toiletries in my arms awkwardly, speaking cautiously. "Grey, could we... can we *not* tell anyone about this?"

She hangs her head and shakes it ruefully, patting me on the arm. "No can do, Tabby. This one is just *too* too good to keep a secret."

Tabitha

*B*lare Wellborn wasn't always this guarded; she was fun and outgoing and loud. But she had a secret, one she was hiding from everyone she cared about—the one thing that brought her the most joy, was the one thing she couldn't tell to anyone.

Blare freezes in the aisle of the store, not sure which direction to head in first. She didn't come for cosmetics, but the glittery display of mascara beckoned her. Man, was she a sucker for new products, and she loved getting dressed up. These days, though, there wasn't much opportunity, and she heaved a loud sigh when she snatched up a hot-pink mascara tube and tossed it in her basket.

Biting down on her lower lip, she studied her choices, not paying any attention when someone brushed past her and bumped into her shoulder, causing her to drop her purse. "Oh!" She gasped, startled. "I'm sorry." Blare was always apologizing, and mentally kicked herself for doing it now. After all, she wasn't the one who had smacked into her.

They both bent down, grabbing at her bag. Hands touching. Fingers grasping. Then, "Oh..." Hazel eyes stared back at her, a tuft of shockingly dark brown locks brushed away by a masculine hand. "Don't apologize. I bumped into you." His voice. His lips. That ruggedly handsome face, those kind eyes. They regarded each other then, something passing between them: recognition. Attraction. Definitely *attraction....*

Leaning back in the high-back chair, satisfied, I hit SAVE on my laptop, pleased with the progress on my second novel.

My. *Second*. Novel.

Two novels that *I* wrote, all by my freaking self.

Me!

A romance writer.

I can hardly believe it, and if someone had told me a year ago that I'd be publishing a book—let alone two—well, I wouldn't have believed them. I might have even laughed in their face. Not very ladylike, I know, but there you have it.

My parents would be shocked. And horrified—not because I've written a book, but because they're fifty shades of smut. I don't even want to imagine what I'd say to my grandparents.

And if Cal found out? I would never live it down.

I grin, imagining the tasteless jokes and innuendos

my brother would throw down if he discovered my secret, but also saddened by the knowledge that I'm hiding it from him, because I know he would support me. Be proud.

My biggest fan.

Ironically, despite his rough exterior and grumpy disposition, Cal has always been my biggest cheerleader. When I was a teenager and became obsessed with animals—stray dogs at the pound in particular—he helped me raise money to donate to the shelter. Together we went to buy pet supplies the shelter needed with the cash I'd raised.

When I went through my boy band phase, it was Cal who went with me to stand in line at the radio station, overnight, to enter a contest for a chance to win tickets.

And every spring when we mulch our parents' landscaping, I always weasel my way out of working in the yard by faking an injury, and he's never *once* ratted me out.

Heaving a loud sigh at the memories, I reach over the side of my chair to root around the tote next to my table for a pen, feeling around inside the bag blindly with one hand and coming up empty. I lean over farther to yank it open and peer inside.

Ah-ha, there it is.

I pop the pen cap off with my teeth and admire the paperback proof for my *first* book—which hasn't even been officially released yet—resting on the table next to my soy latte, trailing my fingers across its sleek cover and glossy design. I turn the paperback this way and that, admiring the two entwined, *naked* bodies in the heat of passion, the shocking red title, and my name in bold letters splashed across the front.

My name!

Well, my pen name, anyway.

A pair of blue ear buds dangle from my lobes and down the front of my white tee shirt, and I reset my music playlist before flipping open the proof copy of my book, pen poised and ready for edits.

Disappointed, the first page—the title page—is pixelated, so I circle it and add a note in the margin for my formatter. Thirty pages in I find a typo, and a few chapters further, too many spaces between paragraphs, a sentence that's meant to be italicized. There are narrow margins in the epilogue.

I circle them all.

I forgo acknowledgements in this book because, well, who am I going to thank?

No one knows I wrote it.

And if none of my family or friends know I wrote it, who's even going to read it? Probably no one. But I didn't write it for them or for strangers; I wrote it for me.

It's something I've always wanted to do; it's always been my passion. My career goals never included working for my parents. Don't get me wrong—I love them to death and I like my job, but…

…the construction company is *their* passion. *Their* vision. *Their* dream.

Not mine.

But my parents count on me—always have—trusting that Cal and I will take ownership of their company when they retire. They have confidence in us, put us through Business School at Ivy League colleges, and rely on us to continue their legacy.

Lately though, for the first time in my life, the

thought of living someone else's dream is stifling me. Suffocating. It might be what my brother wants, but it's holding me back.

I rest my back against the soft cushion, my pen hovering above the cream pages of my novel—all three hundred and eighty pages of it. Setting the blue felt-tip pen down, I trace the title on the cover with my hand, letting my fingers run up and down the glossy surface.

I lift it with both hands and lift it to my nose, inhaling the smell of freshly printed paper and sighing before clutching it to my chest.

This book is my baby. My labor of love. The best thing that's happened to me in years.

And I have no one to tell.

With a sigh, I continue to write.

Blare closed her eyes and tried to remember him. What he looked like, how he sounded, what it felt like when he handed her the discarded mascara that had fallen on the cold tile of the store. He felt familiar to her, like someone she'd known all her life. Like they were connected somehow, and it made her heart beat faster.

Oh well. She wasn't going to see him again. What would be the odds? A million to one? Serendipity only happened in fairy tales, and Blare's life was anything but. With her eyes open and reality surrounding her, the fast-paced beating of her heart gradually returned to normal. But her memory of him never would...

Collin

The pink hat gives her away.

I spot it as soon as I push through the door at Blooming Grounds, a coffee shop in the heart of the city, sandwiched between a hotel chain and insurance brokerage firm. It's surprisingly cozy.

Hefting my black leather laptop bag up and bending at the neck to move the strap over my head, I sling it around my torso, resting the cross-body strap diagonally against my chest.

I hold it steady while I… *study* her.

I hone in on Tabitha Thompson, the brightest spot in the room. It can't be anyone but her—I would recognize that ball cap anywhere. She was wearing it during that embarrassing display she put on last week when she accused my sister of cheating on her brother. With me.

Not that I blame her; my sister and I look nothing alike and Greyson was far from college, home for an impromptu visit.

With her back to me, Tabitha's spine is bent over a glowing laptop monitor, blonde hair in a ponytail she's pulled through the back of her hat.

Baseball caps and ponytails; man, I love that shit.

Cautiously, I approach her from behind, my eyes raking her back. Her bra is visible through her thin white tee, faded cut-up jeans, and navy flip-flops—she looks casual and relaxed. As her fingers fly across her keyboard, the *tap tap tapping* sound resonates, filling the gap of space around the small square table she occupies in the center of the room.

I observe her for a few minutes from across the room until she leans back in her chair, digs in her bag to produce a pen, and eventually begins scribbling in a paperback book.

Inching closer, I watch as she sets the pen down and closes the book to run a hand over its surface, her fingers stroking the cover before raising it to her nose and giving it a whiff. Yeah, you heard me—she's smelling the book.

Who does that?

Then, as if *that* wasn't weird enough, Tabitha grasps the book tightly, clutches it to her chest, and… hugs it?

Uh, okay.

She might be weird, but my looming over her is just as creepy. The soft, dull light from Tabitha's monitor draws me in, and curiously, I hover closely behind her, scanning the paragraph she'd undoubtedly been pounding away on earlier.

Wait. Does that sentence say, *Blare could not stop thinking about him, the guy from the store. His hazel eyes burned holes into her soul and made her center quake. She was experiencing want and desire like nothing…* nothing *she'd ever felt before. She wanted to strip them both naked right there, drag him into a dressing room, and let him—*

Holy shit.

I *feel* my eyes widen in shock. Bugging out of my fucking skull is probably more accurate, because—holy shit—Tabitha Thompson is writing a sex book in the middle of a public coffee shop.

Smut. A bodice ripper.

Whatever the hell you wanna call it.

In disbelief, I give my hair a shake before pushing the black sunglasses up so they rest atop my head. My eyes hit her monitor again, seeking, reading word after suggestive word.

I've seen what I've seen and I can't un-see it.

Drawing even closer, my intention isn't to scare the *shit* out of her, but that's exactly what happens when I let out a surprised gasp. Yeah, I fucking gasp. Like a goddamn girl.

Startled, Tabitha turns.

Her eyes hit my legs first, climb leisurely up my body, pausing on my broad chest, and widen with surprise, then recognition.

Dismay.

The book falls from her hands, landing on the floor with a soft thud on the carpet, and when I bend to scoop it up, her hand darts out and grips my wrist.

"Don't touch it!" Her voice is filled with panic. "Please just leave it."

I rear my hand back and straighten, my eyes flitting to her glowing screen before she glares at me for gawking, and twists in her chair to close the top with a resounding snap.

She tidies up her workspace then spins to face me.

Well, well, well, someone doesn't want me learning any of her dirty little secrets. My eyes dart to the discarded paperback lying facedown on the floor, and for now she's too flustered to pick it up. What's in that damn book that she doesn't want me to see?

"Collin Keller." Tabitha flashes me a fake smile, her

lips pulled tight across her white teeth. "What on earth are you doing here?"

"You don't have to sound so thrilled to see me."

A blush creeps up her neck, and the hot-pink bill of her ball cap creates an unflattering fuchsia shadow on her skin. She has the decency to look embarrassed by her lack of manners.

"I'm sorry, that was rude. It's just that you startled me." Tabitha bites down on her lower lip, takes a steadying breath, and then asks, "So… what *are* you doing here?"

A laugh explodes out of me. "Just can't help yourself, can you? I work in the financial district. It's four blocks up, actually, but I like it in here better than Starbucks. Much warmer and definitely more quiet. I get more work done here." I motion to the laptop draped across my body, giving the canvas bag a pat. "What about you? What brings you to this neck of the woods?"

"I actually live nearby. I… come here often, usually after work, but I didn't have a lot going on at the office today, so… here I am. Earlier than usual." Her shoulders give an apologetic shrug, and she nervously reaches up to adjust the bill of her pink ball cap.

While she's doing that, my eyes flit to the laptop.

A sly smile curls my lips. "What are you working on?"

Tabitha's hands stop, still holding her brim as her bright blue eyes narrow suspiciously for a few seconds, assessing, as if trying to gauge my sincerity.

Like she doesn't quite trust me.

Like she's looking for any clue that I've seen what's written on her screen.

Why yes, Tabitha. *Yes I have*.

I've seen words like *tremble, breathless, stroke*, and *panting* flash across her monitor, burning themselves in my brain—forever. I'll not likely forget them anytime soon, not only because they were sexy, but because *she* was writing them.

Those sexy words came out of *that* sexy girl, and it has me wondering what other thoughts are going through her obviously dirty mind—because I'm a guy and I wonder about shit like that.

And now look how agitated she is.

She suspects I've seen something; it's written all over her beautiful face.

I try not to snicker. "What was it you said you were working on?"

"What am I working on?" she parrots, her brows furrowed in confusion.

"Yeah, it looks like I interrupted something."

Something *smutty*.

Tabitha bites her bottom lip and looks away guiltily. "Um. Work stuff, I guess."

"What kind of work stuff?" This time I *do* snicker.

She closes the notebook in front of her with a scowl and crosses her arms defensively over her chest. "What's with all the questions?"

"Just curious, that's all." I shoulder the weight of my laptop, laying it on the floor next to her table, and lean my elbow on the back of her chair.

I'm so close now I can smell the sweetness of her hair when she fidgets in her chair, kicking up the air around her.

A nervous giggle escapes her lips—her very nicely

shaped, pink, pouty lips. Some people would call them glossy; I'm calling them *juicy*.

Juicy lips I want to suck on.

"Are you coming?" asks my lazy drawl.

"Ex*cuse* me?" Tabitha's mouth gapes in an *O* of surprise and I suppress the urge to say, *Speaking of coming, weren't you just writing about that very same thing only moments ago?*

But I don't. Instead, I say, "Are you coming to my housewarming party?"

"I didn't know you were having one."

Liar, liar, pants on fire.

"Oh, really? Because I'm pretty sure Greyson told me she invited you. Personally."

"She did?"

I study her, the large blue eyes lined in black, the clear, smooth skin flushed from frustration and embarrassment, and the full lips. Letting my gaze linger until she gets uncomfortable with my scrutiny, she finally breaks contact and turns her face towards the bank of windows on the far side of the coffee shop.

I give my chin a scratch. "Yeah. I'm pretty sure she said you were coming."

Tabitha shakes her head in denial, her blonde ponytail swinging back and forth. "I never said that. I said I had to check my calendar."

Gotcha.

"*Ah*, so she *did* invite you to come."

"Please stop doing that."

"Doing what?"

"You *know* what. Using the word..." Tabitha turns back to stare at me, her eyes bright but guarded. "Stop pushing. You're pushing."

"I'm not pushing." I smile. "I just want you to come."

Yeah. You bet your sweet ass I meant for that to sound dirty, and from the look on her face right now, she knows it.

She hesitates before responding, furrowing her brows and eyeing me from under her flirty cap before sliding her notebook off the table and stuffing it into her bag.

Tabitha lifts her laptop, unplugs the earbuds, winding them up along with the power cord, and rises. "I have to go."

My eyes flick to the book on the floor, but morbid curiosity keeps me silent.

She grabs at her phone charger, stepping on it and stumbling when she yanks it up, trying to coil it around her hand. As she abandons tidiness, the black cord gets shoved haphazardly into her brown leather tote, and she shoulders it before grabbing an uncovered, steaming coffee off the table top.

It spills, wetting her hand and soaking the hem of her white shirt.

Her cheeks are beet red when she faces me, barely able to look me in the eye. "It was nice seeing you again."

Tabitha turns, stalks away.

Doesn't look back.

Doesn't see me bend and snap the thick paperback novel up, discarded on the floor.

Doesn't see the expression on my face when I flip it over and crack the cover, or the grin that spreads across my face.

I look up, watching her hurriedly retreating form through the glass, her ass in those ripped up jeans. Tabitha stops at the corner, glancing both ways before crossing to the other side of the street.

Within seconds, she's out of sight.

Gone.

3

Collin

A few hours later, my solitary dinner plate washed and put away, I step into the kitchen to wipe down the cold granite countertop, pausing at the sink to rest my hip against the cabinet.

"The book," as I've started calling it, rests on the kitchen table, cover-side up, the erotic silhouette of a naked couple in all their bare-assed glory for my viewing pleasure. I stride over, gaping down before gingerly lifting it, intently fixating on the suggestive embrace, the full-on kiss, the sweaty bare skin, and the sexy shot of side boob.

Overturning it to read the blurb on the back—studying it for the third time since jamming it into my laptop bag at Blooming Grounds and bringing it home—my eyebrows still shoot damn near into my hairline as I read:

On the Brink, a debut novel by TE Thomas.

Rachel Neumann is a virgin on the brink… on the brink of want, on the brink of curiosity, on the brink of her twenty-first birthday. Rachel wishes for one thing and one thing only: to be ruined. To lose it all in one night of passion… With seduction in mind, there's only one person who can cure her aching body: Devon Parker. He's the only person who has always stood by her, and he's the one person who stirs all her lust-filled desires. Will friends become lovers, or will Rachel always be a virgin on the brink?

Whoa.

Holy shit.

I flip the book over to the front, and I scan the cover again before flicking it open to look inside. Bold, black handwriting and notations are scrawled across the first few title pages in pen:

Too pixelated. Must be 300 dpi, not 199. Change font.

There's no doubt this has to be what she was working on at the coffee shop. I flip the book back over to stare at the author name on the cover:

TE Thomas

It's quite conceivably the *least* creative pen name I've seen. And I've seen—okay fine, I've seen *none.*

But TE Thomas isn't clever at all, especially if she's trying to be covert about it. I mean, come on, TE Thomas? I might be going out on a wild limb here, but it's safe to say her middle name is Elizabeth. If I was a betting man, I would win.

So, this is what she's been hiding.

She's an author.

I take the book into the living room and flop into an overstuffed leather chair, propping my feet up on the coffee table Greyson made me buy. Settling in for the long haul, I crack the novel open to the first chapter and read: *Rachel Neumann was hot, sticky, and panting—and it wasn't from the heat…*

A grin crosses my face as I devour page after page.

Tabitha Thompson, you secretive little sneak.

4

Tabitha

I can *feel* Collin Keller surveilling me from across his living room, his scrutiny so penetrating that sweat begins to dampen my spine.

Great. *Just* what I need.

It's not like I've never had attractive guys notice me before; I've dated my fair share of handsome men. In fact, my last boyfriend was a Minor League Baseball player on his way to the pros, and a total babe.

Hilarious. Smart.

Constantly surrounded by groupies…

Jared would have been perfect if it hadn't been for those damn baseball groupies. No woman wants to listen to their date's phone blow up the entire time they're trying to eat dinner, and no woman wants to see their date's lips tip into a knowing smirk every time he checks a text.

Shady.

But the thing is, Jared never witnessed me on the verge of a public meltdown, never saw me screech like a banshee and react without getting the facts, never saw me stutter out an apology. Never saw me panic and flee from a coffee shop like I had something to hide.

Never caught me writing erotica.

Collin Keller has.

And I'm humiliated.

My gaze swings to him, now that he's *finally* turned his back on me, and trails down the corded column of his long neck—the most erotic part of a man's body, in my opinion—and rests on the silky hair that could use a trim.

Or my fingers running through it.

The solid muscles of his back are outlined by the worn cotton of his clingy tee, and my trajectory aims for his spine. Down. Down to the tapered waist. His ass... *Jesus*. His ass.

Collin Keller is all hard lines and smooth edges.

My mouth waters a little, not gonna lie.

Momentarily, I forget myself and want to see the rich hazel eyes and lopsided grin that made my insides go melty the *second* I found out he was Greyson's brother, and *not* her new boyfriend.

Melty like warm, liquid chocolate.

I bet he tastes just as good.

God, he's so effing handsome.

Still, I made a complete and utter *fool* of myself in front of him two weeks ago, and again last week when we bumped into each other at Blooming Grounds.

When I totally lost my cool... slammed my computer

shut… spilled my coffee… dropped my book… tripped over my power cord.

Ran out on him without saying good-bye. *Who does that?*

I can hardly look the guy in the eye now—and he seems so nice.

Looks so nice.

Nice and yummy.

Guh!

And let us not forget how ridiculously attractive he is.

If only he'd stop looking over here, like he knows a secret. Like I'm… captivating. Like I amuse him. Well, okay, I *am* captivating and amusing, and not without my charms, but he doesn't need to keep *staring* at me like that. It's making me extremely uncomfortable. Not to mention *tingly* in all the right places.

Yeah, *those* tingles.

It's one thing for *me* to gawk at someone, completely another for them to gawk at me. I at least do it from a corner when no one's watching.

Oh. Wait…

I'm going to classify his heated stares as figments of my *very* vivid imagination, which has gotten increasingly more colorful since I started writing my books. *Every* guy, young or old, is a potential character or potential muse. I can now turn everyday occurrences into romance, innocent sentences and questions into innuendo.

Take our run-in at Blooming Grounds, for example, when Collin asked if I was going to be at his housewarming party. He said 'coming,' and immediately my thoughts went to *sex*—lots and lots of sex. Sweaty, sticky, loud sex.

How sick and wrong is that? My deliberately tawdry

mind *went* there willingly, and all the poor guy did was ask an innocent question.

I am a horrible person.

Heat rises in my neck, and I can feel my face get bright red. My only option is to turn and face the snack table, staring down the guacamole dip and willing my heart rate to slow down. I'm not hungry, but I busy myself, grabbing a plastic plate from the stack and piling tortilla chips—*lots* of tortilla chips—then carrots, cucumbers, and celery onto the plate until I run out of room.

I glance down at the bending plate. *Shoot, maybe I overdid it a tad.* Biting down on my lower lip, I stare at the wall—at the artwork he has hanging above the snack table, shifting my attention to his bookshelf.

Curious, I meander over, balancing my plate with one hand and trailing the other along the shelves. Surprised by the diversity of titles, I finger a vintage copy of To Kill a Mockingbird, which is sandwiched in between a biography on John F. Kennedy and the Maze Runner series. There's a colorful row of the same children's Encyclopedias I had growing up, and I crack a nostalgic smile.

I loiter a bit longer and sigh, knowing I should rejoin the group I came here with: Greyson, Cal, and their friend Aaron. The fact that I'm hiding in a corner is absolutely ludicrous; I'm a grown woman.

Nonetheless, I glance over my shoulder.

Yup. Still staring.

Dammit!

Why is he still staring? What is his *deal*?

Rattled by his attention, I stare at my plate, the hairs on the back of my neck prickle, and a tiny, nervous knot takes root in my stomach. When I inhale a deep breath and count to three, raising my head again to meet Collin's eyes, that knot turns into a flutter.

A flutter of excitement.

He doesn't even have the decency to pretend not to be watching me, hoisting his beer glass up in a silent toast, nodding his head towards me in a friendly greeting.

It's his eyes, however, that give him away.

They're perceptive. Insightful. *Kind* but also… shrewd. And he was acting weird at Blooming Grounds. I mean, how many times did the guy say *come* in a sixty-second period? Five? Six?

He *knows* something. I can feel it.

Collin

I lean against my shiny stainless steel oven, arms crossed as I blatantly stare at Cal's sister from across the kitchen of my new condo. I'm half listening to something my childhood friend Dex is saying, and my narrowed eyes bore into Tabitha Thompson as she tucks a loose, dark blonde strand of hair behind her ear, then tips her head back to laugh.

Her throat is tan and graceful and smooth.

Just how I remember it.

Damn, I bet she smells good, too.

Casual in jeans and a plain black tee shirt, there is no mistaking the resemblance between Tabitha and her brother now that they're in the same room together. Both tall with dirty blonde hair, they share the same bright blue eyes and height; but where Cal is hard and rugged—rough around the edges—sporting a perpetual black eye and scarred lip from rugby, Tabitha is all feminine curves and delicate features.

When I said she had a bony ass two weeks ago, I was full of shit.

She's the most fascinating thing I've ever seen.

She writes sleazy romance novels and works for a construction company.

She called me ridiculously good looking—*ridiculously* good looking. What does that even mean?

I continue observing her, waiting for her attraction towards me to manifest itself in some way—a flirty glance in my direction, a coy smile. Shit, I'll settle for *eye* contact.

She's giving me nothing.

If Tabitha Thompson is attracted to me, she sure as shit hides it better than most; she's been avoiding me like the plague since stepping her high-heeled feet through the front door of my condo.

I have to give her props; she's stealthy, that one. I'm talking expert-level evasion. My condo isn't large, but somehow she's managed to elude me like the fiercest competitor in a game of Mortal Kombat.

Not to brag, but I'm fucking *great* at that video game. I will Level 300 that shit against any thirteen-year-old and kick their tech-savvy ass. Oh, Mortal Kombat doesn't have levels, you say? Tough shit. It does when *I* play—I'm so badass I *make* levels.

It's been one week since I bumped into her writing at Blooming Grounds, and two weeks since Grey and I ran into her shopping. But since her arrival at my housewarming party, she's been dodging me, pretending not to be affected by my presence.

Like right now, for example, Tabitha is bearing down on the snack table, staring at the sandwiches and loading up on nachos like she's a waitress in a bar, and it's her job. She's probably not even going to eat any of it; she just doesn't want to turn around and acknowledge me.

As if I wouldn't notice her reluctance to be in the same room. I enter a room, she exits. I move through a room, she crosses to the other side. Cat and mouse.

In my own damn house.

Shit, now she has me rhyming.

This little game of hide and seek is driving me fucking nuts.

"Are you even listening?" An elbow meets my ribcage, jarring me momentarily. Finally nodding at something Dex is saying beside me, I turn towards Cal and rejoin their conversation.

"I'm sorry, what were you saying?"

My sister's boyfriend tracks my movement, looking over at his sister and then at me. He briefly pauses before responding. "I asked Dex if he was coming with you to my match against Purdue in two weeks. He said no."

Dex pulls at the preppy bowtie around his throat. "Can't. My sisters have a thing."

He has sixteen-year-old twin sisters.

"High school musical opening night," he explains. "Shouldn't be too bad. This year they're doing…"

Nodding absentmindedly, I stop listening to watch Tabitha out of the corner of my eye. She leans against the far wall of my living room, balancing a monster plate of chips and veggies while smiling at something my aunt Cindy and cousin Stella are saying. At that moment, her tongue darts out between cherry-red lips to lick the corner of her mouth.

My eyes are riveted.

"Alright, let's cut the crap," Cal's deep voice interrupts, along with another quick jab to my ribcage. "What's going on between you and my sister?"

"Nothing."

He doesn't mince words. "Bullshit. I've been watching you watch her try to get away from you all night."

Strangely enough, I understand every word he just

said. And since he brought it up, I might as well ask. "Yeah, what is *up* with that?"

I cross my arms over my chest resentfully, still staring at Tabitha.

"Okay, I get it now." Cal tips back his beer and swallows hard. "No wonder she didn't want to come."

My head whips around. "What the hell does that mean?"

The bastard laughs drolly. "Grey had to practically *force* her."

"Why?"

He shrugs his broad shoulders. "Because. I guess she's still embarrassed about accusing Greyson of cheating on me with you or some shit. We had to pull out the big guns to get her here."

For fuck's sake. "What's *that* supposed to mean?"

"It means we had to fucking bribe her to come. We knew at some point you'd have to see each other again, and figured she might as well get it over with. Grey swore she'd come home for a girls' night out with Tab's friends. Oh—we also promised her she didn't have to talk to you tonight." He tenderly traces two fingers over his left eye, which is blackened by a fresh bruise and stitched up with black thread. "Still, we literally had to shove her into my truck. I felt like a goddamn kidnapper, minus a disturbing lurker van."

Lovely.

But can I point something out? Two weeks ago she called me ridiculously *good looking*—not to mention, she was totally checking me out at Target. Damn straight she was. Which means she's attracted to me.

Like I'm going to forget *that* little factoid anytime

soon. Not a chance.

Cal taunts, "I mean—just look at her trying to avoid you and shit."

He's right. Tabitha skulks from the snack table to the bookshelf on the far wall of my living room, balancing her loaded plate in one hand and running the other along the wooden shelves. She trails the tips of her fingers across a leather-bound volume of Walt Whitman, then all the way over to a copy of Divergent.

She pops a chip in her mouth, chewing slowly, and stands rigidly, studying the contents of my collection—which isn't that extensive. I'm not a big reader or anything, but I have a few good ones, most of them gifts from my mom, who's always tried to get me to read more. And play Sudoku. Improve my "brain function," like I have all the time in the world for word puzzles and shit.

Also propped on the bookshelf, dead center on the middle shelf not far from where Tabitha is lingering, is her novel, faced out and eye level. All she has to do is take three dainty steps to her left. Three tiny steps or one hundred and sixty degrees to her left, and she'd see it.

Right there, in front of her beautiful face.

I raise the beer bottle in my hand to my lips, sipping with a wide smirk when Tabitha turns her back to the books. Yup, I'm confident she doesn't know I have her paperback proof. Her naughty, *naughty* little novel, all marked up with edits and comments.

I can hardly wait to finish reading the damn thing.

Then tell her about it.

Man, she is going to be *pissed*.

A sick part of me is disappointed, wanting her to turn back around and notice the book; it would force her to confront me. And yeah, it's kind of a dick move to keep it and display it out in the open where anyone could see it, put two and two together—but what are the odds of that happening? Slim to none.

It must be important. And yes, I realize I have to eventually return it, but seriously, what fun would it be to just hand it over?

No. I'm going to make her work for it.

Does that make me a sick bastard, or what?

Blare could hardly believe she was seeing him again. She actually wanted to crawl under a rock and hide. Unfortunately for her, she was trapped in this condo with a group full of people, her ride home no closer to being ready to leave than she had been ten minutes earlier.

She turned, grasping for a fancy bookend she'd managed to knock loose. It fell to the ground with a heavy clang, and when she bent to pick it up, there he was, devouring her with his penetrating stare.

He was staring, watching her from across the room. How had he even ended up here, in this condo?

Wishing she had something to occupy her hands, Blare made a beeline for the food, his image filling her mind as she filled her plate. He was so painfully handsome she could barely stare at him for too long. Why couldn't he have been a jerk at the store? She moved then, closer to the windows, looking down into the bustling city traffic, wishing she were anywhere but here... away from him.

Because he scared the shit out of her.

Why was she avoiding him? Because in a crazy, bizarre twist of fate, the good-looking stranger with the gorgeous, seductive eyes is her best friend's step-brother and completely off-limits. Cheeks flaming hot, Blare plucked a wine glass off a nearby table, and chugged it….

5

Collin: *I have something here that belongs to Tabitha. Can you give me her cell?*

Greyson: *You haven't texted me in days, and now it's only because you want my friend's number?! Rude.*

Collin: *Please? I'll go buy that ugly-ass shower curtain you picked out.*

Greyson: *Fine. Deal. But I'm not giving you her cell—she won't want you having that. You can have her email address instead.*

Collin: *What the hell, Grey? Why not?*

Greyson: *She's still embarrassed about what happened at Target.*

Collin: *So?*

Greyson: *loud sigh You just don't understand women at all, do you...*

Collin: *That's never been up for debate.*

Greyson: *Do you want her info or not?*

Collin: *Fine. Yes.*

Greyson: *I know you're pouting, you big baby.*

Greyson: *Ready? Here it is…*

Greyson: *Don't abuse it. Tell her what you need to tell her, then leave her alone.*

Collin: *Me? Abuse it? It pains me that you would say that. Like I would abuse her privacy like that…*

Greyson: *You WOULD do that.*

Collin: *Yeah, I totally would, but only because I have no boundaries—but not in a weird way.*

Greyson: *I'm confused. What other way is there?*

Collin: *Oh gee, let me think—inventing a fake boyfriend and blasting it on Twitter like some "other people" I know. That's the other way.*

Greyson: *Sometimes I wish I was an only child.*

To: tabtomcat@tthompsoninc.gm
From: CollinKell59@ztindustries.corp
Subject: Thank You

Tabitha, thanks for coming with Cal and Greyson to my housewarming party last night. I hope you enjoyed yourself. Thank you for the bottle of wine. Just a quick note: I have a book that I think belongs to you. Actually, I *know* it does because you left it at Blooming Grounds and I'm just now getting around to letting you know. Let me know how best to return it to you.

CK

To: CollinKell59@ztindustries.corp
From: tabtomcat@tthompsoninc.gm
Subject: ??

Collin. I'm confused. How did you end up with it? I knew I misplaced it, but it never would have occurred to me that you had it since I was just at your house. So now I'm wondering, why didn't you give it back to me then??? I'm sure you've guessed by now that it's important. Would it be an inconvenience for you to pop it in the mail as soon as possible?
    Tabitha Thompson

To: tabtomcat@tthompsoninc.gm
From: CollinKell59@ztindustries.corp
Subject: No can do.

Tabitha, to answer your question, you dropped the book at Blooming Grounds. During your tizzy. And unfortunately, mailing the book won't work for me. Want to meet somewhere? I don't mind getting it to you in person.
    CK

To: CollinKell59@ztindustries.corp
From: tabtomcat@tthompsoninc.gm
Subject: I wouldn't want to impose.

Collin. That's a very generous offer, but to save you trouble, again, why not just pop it in the mail? I'll gladly pay the shipping.
    Tabitha Thompson

To: tabtomcat@tthompsoninc.gm
From: CollinKell59@ztindustries.corp
Subject: No big deal

Tabitha, I can assure you, it would be no imposition. How does 5:30 on Thursday night sound? After work? Does Finches Tap House sound good to you? It's on the corner of Rayburn and Division. CK

To: CollinKell59@ztindustries.corp
From: tabtomcat@tthompsoninc.gm
Subject: Sounds good

Collin. Yes, I know where that is.
You're going to force me to see you... aren't you?

To: tabtomcat@tthompsoninc.gm
From: CollinKell59@ztindustries.corp
Subject: It's a date.

We're on for 5:30. Can't wait.
    CK

To: CollinKell59@ztindustries.corp
From: tabtomcat@tthompsoninc.gm
Subject: Fine.

It's not a date.

Tabitha: *Collin, it's Tabitha Thompson. I hope it's okay that I asked Greyson for your cell. I wanted to let you know that I'm no longer available to meet Thursday.*

Collin: *Not to be rude, but you are full of shit.*

Tabitha: *Why on earth would I lie?*

Collin: *I can think of a couple reasons. 1) because you're embarrassed I witnessed your tantrum at the store, and 2) because you write dirty, dirty books...*

Tabitha: *They are NOT dirty books!*

Collin: *Not dirty? What about this part: "And when he stroked my inner thigh, my body quivered and started on fire, igniting my core." What the hell is a core, by the way?*

Tabitha: *STOP! Just stop. I get the picture. Fine, they're dirty books. Big deal. And anyway, I have a work thing on Thursday I forgot about.*

Collin: *"A work thing." Has anyone told you you're a terrible liar?*

Tabitha: *I honestly CANNOT meet with you on Thursday. Can you just send my book in the mail? Please.*

Collin: *That makes no sense. We live in the same city. Besides, how is that any fun?*

Tabitha: *Fun? I'm not looking for fun. I just want my book back! I'm sure you've noticed it contains notes. It's valuable. The sooner you send it back the better.*

Collin: *Too bad. I'm not sending it in the mail. You have to meet me, or you'll never hold it in your greedy hands again.*

Tabitha: *That's blackmail!*

Collin: *No, it's extortion.*
Tabitha: *Um no… it's blackmail.*
Collin: *Semantics. Text me when you're ready to negotiate.*
Tabitha: *That will NEVER happen. NEVER!!!!*

Tabitha: *Okay, fine. What's it going to take?*
Collin: *Wow, you held out an entire twenty minutes. I expected more resistance from you, quite honestly. This must be driving you crazy, huh?*
Tabitha: *You have no idea.*
Collin: *Oh, I have an idea.*
Tabitha: *Could you please just mail it? Please. I'm asking nicely.*
Collin: *Actually, that sounds more like begging.*
Tabitha: *You're bordering on obnoxious.*
Collin: *Calling me names isn't going to convince me.*
Tabitha: *…and by 'obnoxious' I meant adorable?*
Collin: *Fine, I'll think about it.*
Tabitha: *Really?!*
Collin: *No.*

To: CollinKell59@ztindustries.corp
From: tabtomcat@tthompsoninc.gm
Subject: Clearing the air.

Collin. So, I've been wanting to clear the air since we last met, but have been too nervous. And embarrassed. I never did apologize for what happened when I saw you and Greyson at the store and jumped to conclusions. And for being weird at the coffee shop. And avoiding you at your housewarming party. Wow. Putting it into words really looks… terrible. Yikes! It was all very childish. I'm sorry.
Tabitha

To: tabtomcat@tthompsoninc.gm
From: CollinKell59@ztindustries.corp
Subject: Possession is 9/10th of the Law

If you're trying to get me to change my mind by apologizing, it won't work. Nice try though. Seriously, your mild effort only mildly warms my heart. This reminds me of the time I nailed my sister in the face with a football and the force knocked her flat on the ass. I apologized, but only because my parents made me. And Greyson knew I only said sorry to get myself out of trouble. It worked on my parents, but it won't work on me. You can sweet-talk me *all you want*, but this book is now in a hostage situation. I shall enjoy reading it *again and again and again,* while thinking of you the entire time.
CK

To: CollinKell59@ztindustries.corp
From: tabtomcat@tthompsoninc.gm
Subject: Thinking of me the entire time?

Collin, dear God, please don't—I don't want you

thinking of me AT ALL, let alone the *entire* time you're reading my book. Alright. You've worn me down. Since the book is valuable to me, I agree to meet you Thursday. But just so you know, it's under EXTREME duress. Tabitha

Collin: *TE Thomas, I will see you Thursday.*

Collin

If a glower could kill, I would be a *dead* man.

We're sitting across from each other at a booth at Finches Tap, a slightly grimy sports bar in a rougher part of town, but what Finches lacks in cleanliness it makes up for in atmosphere.

Dimly lit leather booths line the walls, loud music masks chatter from surrounding patrons, and beer is served ice cold. The wait staff is experienced and knows when to disappear.

Like now.

Left alone to our own devices in the seclusion of our giant corner booth, Tabitha and I each have our arms crossed defensively, regarding each other across the marred tabletop like the worthiest adversaries, spoiling for a showdown. Under the hazy overhead light and flickering candle in front of us, Tabitha's glossy lips gleam as her eyes do their best to spear me into silence.

Unsuccessfully, I might add.

I refuse to let her spoil my good mood.

"You know what my favorite part of your *whole* book was—besides the part where Rachel finally loses her virginity? This part here." I poke the open page with my forefinger and slide the book nearer to Tabitha across the table. "This part here, where she asks Devon to be her love coach." I lower my voice to a whisper, conspiratorially. "Did you know by *love*, Rachel actually means…" I look to my left, then to my right, acting covertly like I don't want anyone to overhear me. "*Sex?*"

I do my best to sound appalled.

"I am well aware." Tabitha glares at me from across the booth, holding her hand out, palm up. She's not smiling, but her gorgeous eyes dance with mischief. "Are you done having fun at my expense?" She wiggles her fingers. "Please hand it over."

"Whoa there, grabby hands." I tsk and wriggle my index finger at her, hesitating to hand her book over. "Just hold your horses a minute. I'd like to read out loud from it first, if you don't mind."

"Actually, I do mind."

"Yeah, but the part where he takes her to his family picnic, and they almost kiss behind the shed? Brilliant sexual tension. Now, drawing your attention to chapter ten—"

"I know what chapter ten says, you ass." Her hand flies across the booth to deftly snatch her novel out of my evil clutches, and defensively she cradles the book to her chest like a newborn baby.

I watch as she relaxes and begins fanning out the pages, thoroughly examining them for damage. Her lithe fingers run over the cover, stroking it like the paperback is actually precious cargo.

What a weirdo.

"What the hell are you inspecting it for?"

"You dog-eared the pages!" She accuses me with another pissed-off scowl, her blue eyes squinting at me. Opening a black messenger bag, she carefully digs through it, clears a spot, and strategically places the book inside. "*Why* would you do that?"

"You *wrote* in it!" I pick up a menu that's lying in the center of the table and give her a carefree shrug. "Besides, I didn't have a bookmark."

"You read it?" She gasps, horrified. "You *read* my romance novel?"

"Well, yeah. I like to read, so…" I shrug my broad shoulders again, defensively. "It's not a big deal."

"But it's my proof copy! I mean, the author's copy. For editing," she screeches. The woman in the next booth shushes us. Frustrated, Tabitha lowers her voice. "You don't just *read* a proof copy."

"*You* were reading it," I point out, grabbing a hunk of bread out of the communal bread basket, then peeling the tabs back on two tiny pats of butter. I spread them on before shoving the hunk in my mouth, chewing slowly.

"But it's *mine*. I—" Tabitha clamps her mouth shut.

I swallow before responding. "Wrote it? Yeah, I know." Her mouth falls open. "And you don't trust me with it."

"Look, we could sit here all night—"

"Excellent." I lay down the butter knife and sit back, crossing my arms. Noticing with satisfaction, her eyes follow my movements, up the length of my ripped arms, landing on the hard muscles of my biceps.

I flex.

She rolls her eyes.

"Jeez, would you knock it off? I'm not falling for that." Tabitha gives her head an agitated shake, her silky blonde hair floating around her shoulders in waves. "And stop trying to bait me into an argument."

"Bait you? *Bait* you? What the…" Realization sets in. "*Ahhhh*, a slutty romance book word. I like it."

Her forehead lands with a thud onto the tabletop. She lets out a loud, tortured groan. "Oh my god."

"Don't be embarrassed," I soothe. "It's a really good book. Sort of." I lift the menu, scanning the appetizers. "I mean, it's not winning any Pulitzer Prizes for literature, but I *did* particularly like the part where Rachel finally loses her virginity. It took long enough though—more than halfway into the book? Come *on,* Rachel, show some hustle."

"We are *not* having this conversation."

She's so cute.

"Look, all I'm saying is, Rachel could have shown more sense of urgency. Wasn't the whole point of the book for her to get laid?"

Tabitha lifts her head and wrinkles her nose—her adorable, pert little nose. "No, that wasn't the point of the book, and you do *not* get to give feedback on the plot. It's bad enough that you know I wrote it. I don't even know how you knew."

"Seriously, Tab? I would think that was pretty obvious. I mean, your pen name is basically your name, so..."

"It is not!"

"Tabitha Elizabeth Thompson. TE Thomas? *Really*? What kind of a moron do you think I am?"

"No one is supposed to know." She says it in such a small voice I have to strain to hear her across the noisy din of Finches.

"What do you mean no one is supposed to know? Does your family know?" I lay my palms flat on the table. "It's awesome that you wrote a book. Tabitha—you *wrote a book*."

She's silent, so I continue. "Help me understand why someone beautiful, intelligent, and so obviously clever would hide the fact that she wrote a novel. Why won't you tell people?"

She hides her face in her palms and mumbles, "Because. It's embarrassing."

As if that explains everything.

"What is?"

She sits up straighter then and blows out a frustrated little puff of air, causing delicate wisps of light blonde hair to float around her face. She tilts her head back, and it hits the red leather back of the booth. After staring at the ceiling for a few heartbeats, Tabitha raises her head and looks me directly in the eye. "If I hadn't written a romance, I would probably tell people. Maybe if the book wasn't as explicit as it is. But I don't want my parents to know I wrote something so..."

Her hands come up and do this little lilty thing in the air that girls do when they can't find the right words to finish a sentence.

I decide to help her out. "Porn-ish?"

"No! It's not porn, it's…" Again with the hand waves.

"Whore-ish?"

"No! Collin, stop." A smile teases her lips and her eyes, well—those are gazing at me all wide and sparkly. Laughing. Fucking intense is what those gorgeous eyes are, and they're directed at me. "It's… it's…"

"Literotica?"

This stops her train of thought and she looks at me, her face twisted up in obvious confusion. "Wait. *What*?"

"What? You've never heard of Literotica and you *write* it?" She shakes her head slowly. "Don't worry, I hadn't either. It popped up in the search results when I Googled your pen name."

I pick up the water glass and calmly slurp through the straw. The sound makes Tabitha scowl. "Anyway, it's basically written to turn people on. Like porn. But you know—in writing."

"I was going to say that my writing is risqué." Tabitha rolls her eyes; they appear even bluer on her blushing, bright red face. "My book is *not* erotica. That's not what it's about and you know it. Stop making fun of me. It has an actual *plot*, and a storyline, and a climax."

A snort escapes my nose.

"Without trying to get myself into *deeper* trouble, can I just point something out?" I lift the menu again to study the entrées, casually perusing it before coolly pointing out the obvious. "You just said climax."

Her arms go up in defeat. "See? This is why I can't tell my family! Put that menu down!"

Holding the menu *higher*, I block out the glacial stare I know is being directed my way. Her exasperated voice drifts over the top with a huff, and she gives the plastic menu a poke with her finger to regain my attention.

"Would you put down that menu? Collin Keller, we are *not* staying for dinner."

Shit. I kind of like it when she says my name like that, all pissed off and agitated. *Collin Keller, we are not staying for dinner*! So fucking cute.

I put down the menu and pretend to be confused. "But it's dinner time. Aren't you hungry?"

She rolls those gorgeous, baby blues again. "I had a late lunch. On *purpose*."

What a fiery little hothead she is.

I like it.

My fingers drum the tabletop in thought. "So I've been thinking, I know you said you don't consider this a date, but—"

"Hold it right there." Her palm goes up to stop me from finishing my sentence. "This is not a date. A date is getting dressed up, going somewhere nice, and getting to know someone."

"Kind of like what we're doing right now?"

"That is *not* what we're doing right now. Right now we are making an *exchange*."

I disagree and it shows on my face. "What do I get in return?"

"Nothing. I get my book and you get nothing."

"Well, gee, when you put it that way… my end of the deal sounds shitty."

We're interrupted at that moment by the waiter, who steps forward with his pad of paper, pen hovering at the ready. "Have you decided on anything yet, or do you need a few minutes?"

I expect Tabitha to grab her messenger bag and slide her sexy self out of the booth, but instead, she surprises me by grabbing her menu with a resigned huff, scanning it briefly, and saying, "I'll have the black angus cheeseburger, medium rare, with a side of fries. Extra pickles. Oh, and an iced tea please."

She sighs and hands the waiter back his menu. "You made me come here. This is what you get in exchange."

"A non-date date?"

She folds her arms across her fantastic breasts. "*Exactly*. I'm just not sure dating you would be a good decision for *either* of us."

I watch her the entire time I give my order to the waiter. "Double cheeseburger medium rare, cheese curds, ranch on the side." I hand the menu over, Tabitha's earlier agitation making me chuckle. "Why isn't dating me a good decision? And why do you have to say it with that look of disgust on your face. I'm kind of insulted."

"Several reasons, and I'll gladly list them off for you. First, you're Greyson's brother—you don't think that's weird?"

"I refuse to discuss it. *Next*." I watch the kitchen's service door swing back and forth, willing the food to come out though we just placed our orders.

I'm fucking starving.

And not just for food.

Tabitha prattles on across from me. "Second, we got off on the wrong foot. I freaked out at the coffee shop, and now this dating thing could be awkward for us."

"Quit bringing that shit up. Trust, me, you'll get over it. I did. *Next*."

Now she's ticking items off on her fingers, bobbing

her cute little head as she counts. "Third, you just moved back into the area. Don't you want to see what's on the market? There are a lot of attractive women in this city."

"Been there, done that. *Next!*" Shit, maybe I said that one a little too loudly—the couple at the neighboring table crane their necks in our direction.

"You're really annoying."

I ignore her complaining. "Are you looking forward to dinner? I'm *ravenous*." I chuckle, delighted with my own wit. "How's that for smut romance lingo?"

"Meh." She gives me a flirty little wink. "Not bad."

I take that as a good sign. "How bout a glass of wine?"

She sighs, defeated. "I guess I could use some alcohol to calm my nerves, but wine doesn't really go with a burger. How 'bout a beer?" Tabitha reaches for her water, taking a dainty sip before continuing. "You don't want to play the field? Casually date?"

"What am I, nineteen? No." I reach for her hand across the table and pull it towards me. She lets me. "Look, we could do this all night, Tabitha. But I'd rather just enjoy your company." She bites down on her plump lower lip. It's driving me crazy. "God, I can't even look at you without wanting to put my mouth on you."

"Oh my god, you can't just say things like that!" she hisses, mortified.

"You're kidding me, right? You write *sex* books for a living."

"Shh! No one is supposed to know that." Her hand settles into mine and her thumb begins distractedly stroking my palm. "And that's not what I do for a living."

"But that is what you *want* to be doing, right?"

She frowns. "What I want and what's best for me are two totally different things. I can't leave my dad's business until Cal is ready to take on more responsibility."

"Is that what your parents told you?"

"Well, no—"

"And you don't think they want you to be happy, Tabitha?"

When I say her name, she looks up from our joined hands. "Have you always just done what you wanted? As if it were easy?"

"Honestly? Yes."

She bites down on her lip again and gives her head a gloomy little shake. "I thought working for my parents was what I always wanted. It's the only thing I knew." She scoffs. "Hell, my degree is in Business with an emphasis on Construction Management, for crying out loud. It's the only thing I'm qualified for. How sad is that?"

"You're incredible. I am actually in awe of you right now."

"Collin, stop." She tugs her hand out of my grip and sets it in her lap.

"Why should I? You need to hear it."

"I do hear it. My family tells me they love me all the time."

I disagree. Being told you're loved and being given the chance to make your own choices are *not* the same thing, but I keep that opinion to myself, choosing my next words wisely. "Then why are you hiding yourself from them?"

For a while, I don't think she's going to respond. Instead, her forlorn frown studies her hands, where she's clasped them in her lap. Opening her palms, she spreads them wide, appearing, for the first time since I met her, young and vulnerable. "It's because I'm scared."

"Of what?" My words come out above a whisper.

"Of everything."

I pause. "Well, that's horseshit."

Surprised laughter bursts from her lips. "You're ridiculous," she says, shaking her blonde hair. "And kind of an ass."

"You'll get used to it."

And when she does, she'll like it.

Tabitha

I'll be the first one to admit I'm actually enjoying myself on this non-date. Of course, I won't be admitting that to anyone out loud anytime soon. Or in writing.

Well, okay—*maybe* in writing. After all, I still need a storyline for my second book, and Collin makes the perfect muse for the hero: strong, handsome, charming…

Tenacious. Disarming. Alluring.

I sip this disgusting beer and sigh, watching him retreat to the men's room, my rapt gaze trailing after and landing on his tight, firm, denim-clad ass. He's been incredibly attentive, respectful (sort of, for the most part), and funny. Intelligent. Not to mention really, really ridiculously good looking.

Crap.

Now I sound like freaking Derek Zoolander.

And I mentioned he's funny, right? It's a pretty lethal combination, and if he weren't Greyson's brother… and I hadn't acted like a complete bitch when we first met, well…

There might be a slight chance I'd date him.

Oh, who am I trying to kid? I'd date the *shit* out of him in a heartbeat because nice, funny, respectful guys aren't easy to find. In fact, they've become more of an urban legend than a reality.

However, the fact remains: he *is* Grey's brother, and for whatever reason, I find the thought of dating him a bit strange. Weird. Creepy, even.

For me, it feels like fishing for a boyfriend in the family pond.

You just don't do it.

I give myself a pep talk, reminding myself to quit gushing. This thing with Collin Keller is not happening...

I will say this though: he's going to be hard to resist.

Fortunately, I deal with impossible, sometimes arrogant, men at work on a daily basis, so his persistence should be a piece of cake.

Theoretically.

I'll just enjoy his company tonight, and in the future we can causally bump into each other at family functions. This attraction thing is no big deal; I can handle it. I am a fortress of feminine willpower. I've taken all the feminist classes in college. Women's Studies. How to be an Independent Woman 101.

I'll plop Collin deftly into the Friend Zone category, right where he belongs, and that will be that.

It won't be weird at all.

Yup, *that's what I'll keep telling myself.*

The waiter comes with our food and refills while Collin is in the bathroom, and to busy myself, I prep my burger, adding the garnishes and extra pickles. Dipping the burger in ketchup, I take a huge bite and chew.

It's so delicious I actually whimper into my next bite.

My thoughts stray to Collin, and I shake my head. *Get a grip, Tabitha. He is not the guy for you. If you get close to him, the carefully erected wall you built will come crashing down around you...*

I'm so committed to *not* falling under his spell, I avoid looking directly at him when he re-approaches the booth and drops himself down with a cheeky grin. A grin full of white teeth. I don't look away quick enough and can't help but notice one of his bottom teeth is just a tad bit crooked.

Irresistible.

So irresistible that my stomach does that fluttering thing again, followed by my annoying, rapidly beating heart.

Sweaty palms.

A nervous giggle, and I slap a palm over my mouth, horrified. My traitorous body apparently belongs to a hormonal teenage girl.

It has terrible timing.

B*lare twisted a lock of her brown hair and regarded Adam from across the booth, her eyes riveted on his full lips and five o'clock shadow. His words sent shivers down her spine every time he opened his mouth to talk—a mouth she wanted all over her body. Of course, she couldn't admit this out loud—not until she knew how he really felt. He smiled again and laid his palms flat on the table. "Stop teasing me," Blare said, giving her brunette locks an agitated shake, her silky hair floating around her shoulders in waves. "You're trying to bait me into an argument, Adam, and it won't work."*

"Bait you*? What the hell does that even mean?" The dawning of realization sets in and Adam laughs, rich and*

deep and throaty. A laugh that makes Blare want to climb across the table on all fours and straddle his lap. "Ah, a word from one of those slutty romances you're always reading. I like it." He winks at her and she drops her head onto the tabletop with a loud thump, letting out a groan. How humiliating. "Oh my god.".

To: CollinKell59@ztindustries.corp
From: tabtomcat@tthompsoninc.gm
Subject: Thank you. Again.

Collin, thank you for bringing my book back, and for dinner last night. I'm sorry the check ripped in half when I grabbed it, trying to split the bill with you. If I'd known you had the world's strongest vise grip, I wouldn't have bothered.
    Tabitha

To: tabtomcat@tthompsoninc.gm
From: CollinKell59@ztindustries.corp
Subject: You're welcome. Again.

Tabitha, don't worry about it. I'm sure the waiter enjoyed

taping the whole thing back together after we left. Know what he probably enjoyed even more? Seeing you slap my hand away when I tried helping you out of the booth. The expression on his face was priceless.

CK

To: CollinKell59@ztindustries.corp
From: tabtomcat@tthompsoninc.gm
Subject: Helped me out of the booth?

I think you're remembering it wrong. You weren't trying to HELP me out of the booth. You were trying to touch my ass—the SAME ass you called BONY only two weeks prior. *Now* what do you have to say for yourself?

Tabitha

To: tabtomcat@tthompsoninc.gm
From: CollinKell59@ztindustries.corp
Subject: Your ass?

I'll admit, I was hasty in my judgment of your ASSets. Your rear is in no way bony. Especially in those black yoga pants you had on last night. I realize it was your attempt to appear dowdy and less attractive, but you failed miserably. Those pants did nothing but showcase your second best feature.

CK

Collin: *You're adorable when you're nervous.*

Tabitha: *What are you talking about? When was I nervous?*

Collin: *I'm thinking about dinner the other night, when I came back from the bathroom. When you tried to mask your laugh. You shouldn't have covered it up.*

Tabitha: *I wish you wouldn't say things like that.*

Collin: *What things?*

Tabitha: *Charming things that make me question my resolve.*

Collin: *You're thinking way too much. Why can't you just act like a big girl and do what you want? Or better yet, act like a guy and straight up don't give a shit.*

Tabitha: *Because you're Greyson's brother.*

Collin: *What the hell does that have to do with anything? I'm a grown man. I started living for myself years ago.*

Tabitha: *Do I have to spell it out for you????*

Collin: *Yes. And while you're at it, spell out a few naughty words too. I know you know lots of those.*

Tabitha: *Knock it off. I am not sexting you.*

Collin: *That's disappointing. For a sex book author, you're kind of a prude.*

8

Tabitha

"So you think he's into you?" my best friend Daphne asks, propping the popcorn bucket on her legs and balancing it when she reaches to grab her soda off the sofa table.

Tonight is movie night at her place, and I grab the remote for the Blu-ray player, pointing it at the big screen hanging on her living room wall. Skillfully, I click through the menu, find Netflix, and choose How I Met Your Mother. (Does anyone besides me still watch this show?)

"Definitely. We literally argued about why it's a bad idea to date."

"I don't understand how the two of you ended up having dinner together in the first place. Didn't you say you just bumped into him at Target? How'd you end up at

Finches Tap? I don't get it."

So here's the thing. I haven't exactly told any of my friends about the books, either. Especially not Daphne. Don't get me wrong—I love her to death, and we've been friends almost our entire lives, but she wouldn't be able to keep this secret to save her soul. She'd be way too proud and want to tell the entire world!

Daphne is an incredible, loyal friend—but I know eventually she'd spill the beans, and I need my secret to stay hidden.

I hate the lying, but I do it anyway. "Greyson left a textbook at Collin's new condo during his housewarming party, and we met so he could give it to me. Cal's coming home tonight and he's swinging by my place on his way back."

Daphne nods, popping a kernel into her mouth.

In front of me, my cell phone—set on vibrate—begins a jaunty little dance across the wooden coffee table, the buzzing sound oddly shrill in my friend's tiny apartment. The LED lights up.

Collin Keller's name flashes across the screen.

Holy. Moly.

I stare at it, stunned. Why is he calling me? Why. Is. He. Calling. *Me*?

Popcorn spills onto the carpet when my best friend dives off the couch like a rocket, snatching my phone. "Shitballs, is that him? He's calling! No one makes phone calls anymore!" Her hands fly out to stop me from grabbing the phone, but then she tosses it at my chest. I barely catch it, fumbling as Daphne continues shouting at me. "Don't answer it. Wait, answer it! Hurry!"

I smack her hand away. "Shh, would you be quiet!"

Laughing, I answer the phone.

"Hello?"

I hear heavy breathing, followed by a tentative, "Tabitha? Hi. It's Collin. Uh, Collin Keller."

I point to the phone, mouthing, *Oh my god! It's him!* to Daphne, who's now bouncing up and down on the couch like a child, popcorn spilling everywhere. And by everywhere, I mean everywhere—the cushions, the carpet, the table—all littered with fluffy, buttery kernels.

What a flipping mess.

Daphne bounces and looks exactly how I feel—like a teenager, bubbly and giddy and ridiculous.

"I know who this is, you goof." I smack a palm to my forehead. Goof? Ugh. Unsexiest word ever. Daphne titters and tosses a kernel of popcorn into her open mouth, sitting back on the couch and watching me like a television show.

"I hope I'm not interrupting anything?" Surprisingly, he sounds self-conscious.

I glance down at my gray sweatpants, maroon Ivy sweatshirt, and polka-dot fuzzy socks. "Uh, no. It's fine. You caught me just as I was about to climb into a bubble bath."

Daphne raises her eyebrows and snorts. *What*? I shrug. *I'm just giving him a visual of me climbing into the tub. Naked.* Everybody knows that's basic How To Drive a Guy Wild 101: Give him a visual.

"Really?" Is it just my imagination, or did his voice just crack a little?

"Yeah, but don't worry. I'll just take the phone in the tub." Daphne rolls her green eyes towards the ceiling then makes the universal *you're insane* gesture with her hands.

"What are you doing the rest of the night?"

"Um, I'll probably have a glass of wine and sit out on the deck with my laptop." Now my best friend is shaking her head back and forth at me, clearly disgusted. *I'm sorry!* I mouth, while pantomiming, *I can't tell him I'm chilling in sweatpants!*

She sticks her tongue out, sitting cross-legged on the couch. I find my manners and ask him about himself. "What about you? What are you up to?"

Collin thinks about it for a second, static filling the silence. "Not much. There's a How I Met Your Mother marathon on that I'll probably watch."

I freaking love that show.

"You do?"

Shit, did I say that out loud? "Yes. Love, love, love."

"*Say love one more freaking time,*" Daphne whispers. I swat my arm towards her. *Shut up, Daph!*

"Do you..." Collin clears his throat. "Wanna come over and watch it with me? You can sit on one side of the sofa and I'll sit on the other. I'll even let you put your stinky feet on my new coffee table."

Ugh, he is so sweet. I make an *aw* face at Daphne.

"I'd love to, but I really need to stay in tonight." I glance over at my best friend, who's watching me intently. Lowering my voice, I walk towards the kitchen, away from her intense eavesdropping. Peering over my shoulder, I check to make sure she's not listening. "Um, remember I told you I started a second book? I should probably get some of that done since I'm on a roll lately."

"Ah, because I'm your muse." He says it so confidently, like he knows. Damn him. "Bring your laptop over and I'll let you follow me around, observing me in my wild habitat."

I laugh softly, biting my bottom lip to stop the grin spreading across my face. "Collin Keller, you're becoming a real pain in my backside."

He hums through the phone. "You're a breath of fresh air. With a lovely backside."

I shiver. "Collin, don't make this hard."

"Um…" His low hum trails off suggestively. "Too late."

"Oh my god. No."

"Come on, Tabitha, admit it—your mind went there, too."

His voice when he says my name, though… *Ugh*. I love it. I can't resist flirting with him just a little, and if this phone had a cord I'd be twirling it around my finger. "Yours went there first. Besides, it's a hazard of the trade. I can't help playing out scenes in my head."

His laughter is filled with humor. "Just admit it; you have a filthy mind."

"Filthy? That might be a bit of a stretch. I prefer to call it *imaginative*."

"That brings me to the actual reason I'm calling. Let me take you and your imagination out on one date." He's quiet. "Just one."

Daphne is perched on the edge of the couch, spellbound, mouth agape. I point to the phone, mouthing, *He just asked me out*! Then I shoo her to be quiet when she loudly hisses, "*You freaking better say yes*!"

Feigning indifference, I relent. "You know what? Okay. Fine. I give up."

Collin's low chuckle on the other end sends another shiver up my spine. "Okay fine? I give up? Calm down, Thompson, or I might think you actually like me."

"It sounds like you're pouting. Are you pouting, Collin?"

"No comment."

Before I can stop myself, I say, "Aw, you're kind of adorable. Did you know that?"

This cheers him up and I can virtually *hear* him smiling. "Two dates."

"Don't push your luck. Let's just start with one…"

"Can't blame a guy for trying."

Collin: *Hey blondie. Write anything good last night?*

Tabitha: *Actually, yes! A few more chapters in the new book. Plus I'm done editing the proof for On the Brink, book one.*

Collin: *Be honest. You ARE using me as a muse. For real.*

Tabitha: *Why would I do a thing like that?*

Collin: *Because I'm charming and ridiculously good looking. Besides, I noticed you're not denying it.*

Tabitha: *LOL knock it off. I can't get anything done with my phone blowing up every ten seconds.*

Collin: *Give me one line from your new book and we can both get back to work. Promise.*

Tabitha: *Fine. Here it is: "The quiet way she spoke was louder than the words she could have shouted."*

Collin: *Holy shit, that's amazing! You're amazing!*

Tabitha: *blushes Now go back to work.*

Collin: *Fine, but I'm going to be thinking of you all day. I hope you're satisfied.*

Tabitha: *Alright, well—I guess I'll see you soon?*
Collin: *Tomorrow night. Six o'clock?*
Tabitha: *Yes. 6:00.*

9

Tabitha

What was so wrong with him knowing? Blare mulled the question over in her mind at least a few dozen times as she sat in her apartment, wondering what it meant for him to know her secret.

It wasn't like he was going to tell anyone. She liked him—really liked him. Trusted him. Longed for him. Blare finally admitted to herself that it felt good that someone finally knew; the burden of her secret had been lifted off her shoulders, and she didn't have to keep lying anymore. Well, she did, but not to everyone. Not to him. Blare felt freer than she had in years now that someone else knew. And now he was taking her out. On a date. For Blare, the future seemed infinite...

Deftly, my fingers fly across the keyboard on my laptop, and I hesitate. Should I delete any of those few sentences? Will any of them give me away if someone I know reads it? Oh, who am I trying to kid—the only person reading my work is Collin, and he's not saying anything to anyone.

Is he?

I scoff at this notion, deeming it absurd. Quickly, I make myself a note in the margin of my book document, hit SAVE, close my laptop, and stand.

Walking to my closet, I throw open the door and brace my hands on both sides of the doorway, wearing only a nude colored bra and matching underwear. I study my selection of clothes before going in, and head right for the dresses.

Pulling out a gorgeous emerald-green wrap dress, I hold it against my body, running a hand down the length of the fabric and deciding it's the perfect dress for this date.

The color is rich and jewel toned, and sets off the flush of my skin and the blonde of my hair. I've never worn it—never had an occasion—so the tags still hang, dangling from the sleeve. I carefully tug them off and toss them in the garbage under my bathroom sink.

And I might be lying to my family and my friends about what I do in my free time after work, but I won't lie to myself about this date.

I am excited.

No.

No, there has to be a better word for it than *that*…

Euphoric. Nervous? Elated. My body is positively humming with anticipation.

I flatten one hand on my stomach, putting pressure there to quell the nerves taking root, inhale, steadying my breath, and hang the green dress on a hook by the shower. Deep breath, Tabitha. *In through the nose, out through the mouth.*

Why am I so nervous? My hands go to my face; my cheeks are burning. Positively on *fire*.

God, I'm burning up—for *him*.

I feel like…

I feel like this is the start of something momentous. Like the minute I walk out that door, my life is going to change.

Is that weird? Crazy? Melodramatic much?

Who cares! I'm twenty-four years old, for crying out loud. Old enough to be facing this date more logically—instead of like a ditzy sixteen-year-old headed out on her first date.

First date.

First kiss.

First… everything.

With Collin Keller, of all people.

After flipping on the light switches surrounding the vanity at the sink, one by one until the whole room is ablaze, I pull out the stool usually kept under the counter, and sit.

Studying myself in the mirror, I debate how to make over my face. Dramatic look or simple? Dewy or matte?

Smoky or—guh! What the hell am I even saying?

Yes, now I do sound crazy!

My blonde hair is up in giant rollers, and I leave them to cool while applying makeup, my nervous hands shaking when I try to brush on my mascara, careful not to clump it up, and I just barely manage not to stab myself in the retinae. *Barely*.

I brace my hands against the counter, take a few steadying breaths, and stare at my reflection before tackling the mop of thick hair piled on my head.

The rollers come out one at a time, and the blonde waves loosely fall down around my shoulders. I add styling cream to eliminate the flyaways, and set it.

Once that chore is done, I fish around my makeup drawer for the dark plum matte lipstick Greyson gave me for my birthday—she calls it her "lucky gala lipstick"—swipe a few times across my pout, and then give them pucker.

Transformed, I stare.

Give my locks a shake.

Inhale, exhale.

Decision made: I won't resist him anymore if he wants to keep taking me out. If he wants to email and text and talk on the phone. If he wants to take me to bed. I won't resist him at *all*. Doing so would be foolish, and I am no fool. Yes, the lying needs to stop.

I'm going to start by admitting how Collin Keller *really* makes me feel.

He makes me feel clever and funny.

He makes me feel desirable.

He makes me hopeful.

Ugh. How annoying.

Collin

I cannot physically make myself stop staring.

Tabitha is gorgeous.

I give her another sidelong glimpse across my car, my eyes appreciatively scanning her silky legs, demurely crossed at the ankles. The slit in her dress slides open at that exact moment to reveal a sliver of tan thigh.

Focus on the fucking road, Collin, *Jesus*.

Clearly I've completely given up playing it cool.

I'm nervous as hell.

As I white-knuckle the steering wheel, my palms actually begin *sweating*, not just because Tabitha and she's stunning, but because of what I have planned. She's either going to love it or… never want to see me again.

Or slap me across the face, which, to be honest, would be hot as hell.

She's given me one date. One chance. The last thing I want to do is fuck it up. However, I wanted to pull out all the stops without having to ask my sister for advice, and this was the only way I knew how.

Life imitating art.

Her first book.

The chapter I used as inspiration for tonight's date burns, imprinted in my brain.

God, those eyes. Those shoulders. That ass. Would

she ever get sick of watching it walk away? Not in this lifetime... Rachel tried to hide the smile threatening to escape, raising her Chardonnay and studying it. She swirled it then watched as the clear gold liquid crept down the side of the glass, clinging to life. Rachel lowered it then returned it to the table, and watched as Devon reapproached. The butterflies in her stomach flitted and danced carelessly, unaware of the turmoil they caused. These feelings—they weren't part of the plan; she wasn't supposed to fall for him this way... she wasn't supposed to fall for him at all. *The room he'd reserved was intimate, down a narrow hall in the back of the dimly lit Italian restaurant, meant for private parties. Three roses sat in a thin vase in the center of their table: red, yellow, and peach. Roses that Devon had placed there himself. The chardonnay. The way he'd found out and ordered her favorite foods... It was all so perfect. But what did it mean? Rachel was both anxious—and scared—to find out...*

I push her written words out of my mind. What's done is done.

Love it or hate it, there's no turning back now.

Having reached our destination, I easily find a parking spot, pull in, and shift my black sports car into park. I throw open my door and hop out hurriedly, bending at the waist and sticking my head back inside the car to peer in at her. "Don't. Move."

I jog around to the passenger seat and pull the passenger side door open. Tabitha's long, smooth legs appear first, nude high heels hitting the pavement with a tap. My hand reaches for her, and she grasps it, allowing me to assist her out of the car.

The wind throws up a gentle breeze, lifting her hair at the nape of her graceful neck and parting the hem of her dark green dress, à la Marilyn Monroe.

Thank you, wind gods, for that complimentary peep show, although not enough peep to glimpse the goods.

Damn, no such luck.

Tabitha tucks a small purse—handbag, I think girls call it—under the crook of her arm, then runs her hands down her dress, flattening out the wrinkles caused by the wind. She adjusts the sash around her narrow waist, and I notice her flowy dress has a blessedly plunging neckline, exposing an entire eyeful of cleavage that makes my fingers itch.

Of course, I can't help but admire her amazing tits.

Sorry, I mean *breasts*. But come on: They. Are. Right. *There*. The low-cut neckline is an invitation for my eyes to ogle away.

To be completely honest, I'm shocked she's wearing this dress. This dress means she considers this a real date; this is not a dress you wear when you're Friend Zoning a guy. It's a sexy-ass dress you're able to untie with only a gentle tug to the sash. One you drop to the floor at the end of your date.

The kind of dress you wear when you want him undressing you with his eyes all night.

And tonight, it's damn good to be Collin Keller.

The fabric is flirty, silky, and light—touchable *everywhere*. My eyes wander, my hands impatient to shove her back in my car, drive her back to my place, and screw her brains out until she can't remember a single reason we shouldn't be here together—and give her a million screaming reasons why we should.

As my eyes rake over her cleavage, again, I wonder if she's wearing lingerie underneath and what it looks like. My hand settles at the small of her back to guide her towards the restaurant—and hell if it doesn't graze her ass while I'm checking it out.

Damn fine ass.

Makes me wanna slap it, too.

Mind out of the gutter, Keller.

Inside, we're greeted by the hostess.

"Hi," I start, clearing my throat. Here goes nothing. "Party of two for Neumann. That's N-E-U-M-A-N-N. Not to be confused with New Man."

Sadly, the hostess's features remain stoic, not getting my joke and ruining all my fun. Nodding, she motions for us to follow, leading us to the back corner of the restaurant, taking a left to steer us down a hallway. Tabitha glances at me over her shoulder, puzzled, so I feign a shrug, pleading ignorance.

Shit. I hope this wasn't a mistake.

"Here you go, sir. The private room you requested." A door opens and the room we enter can only be described as opulent. Lavish. In the center of the secluded dining room, beneath an ornamental crystal chandelier, is a single set table. Draped white linens cover the surface. Candles and a crystal vase of four long-stem roses occupy the center: red, peach, yellow, and lavender. Several steaming plates of Tabitha's favorite foods have already been served.

The hostess hangs back. "Your sommelier will be back shortly with the Chardonnay."

Tabitha's head rears towards me and her smoky eyes widen, appearing a shocking shade of blue. "Collin, what on earth…"

"Now, Rachel, before you say anything, don't overreact."

"Why are you calling me Rachel? What… Oh, sweet Jesus." She looks around, confused. "Did you..? Wait. Is this what I think it is?"

"No?"

Her eyebrows shoot up into her hairline, skepticism written all over her face. I can't tell if she wants to smack me or not. "Collin Keller, what is going on? Is this the date scene from the paperback proof you stole?" She whispers this last part. "Be honest."

"Okay, yes. This is what it looks like. Are you mad?"

She gives pause, sets her purse down on the table, and then rewards me with a smile when I pull the chair out for her, a gentlemanly gesture that has her blue eyes softening.

I know I've got her.

Score one for Team Collin.

Nervously, she pushes a few strands of hair behind her ear. Sparkling green emeralds shine in her lobes. "I don't even know *how* to be furious with you right now. I'm speechless. Later it might be possible that I'll want to kill you, but right now… I can't even believe you did this."

This is the recreation of the first date scene from her very first book.

This is me romancing a girl who's making it damn near impossible to romance her.

But I'm sure going to fucking try.

10

Tabitha

"Give me your best line." Collin watches me from across the table, taking a forkful of steak and chewing slowly. "Tell me something you've only put on paper. In one of your books."

"It's only the *one* book, remember? Well, two. But the second one is just... me playing around."

He rolls his eyes, still chewing. "Let's assume there will be more."

It's right then that my chest swells and my heart begins beating wildly. Becomes huge. His words release a spark of affection inside me that I can feel—actually *feel*—blossoming into something bigger.

Something wonderful.

Collin believes in my dream.

Collin believes in… *me*.

I could leap across the table and kiss him all over his beautiful, sexy, freshly shaven face.

I bet he smells good. All sexy and mannish.

Collin breaks the silence. "Well? If you can't think of one, I can supply one for you. Confession time: I read your proof *three* times before giving it back to you. I've got a few good zingers locked away up here." He taps his skull with a forefinger, saying it so casually I have to replay it in my mind a few times.

"*Three times*!" I sputter ineloquently. "Why?"

"Because it was good?" He lays his fork on his dinner plate and leans forward, resting his elbows on the table. "Mostly I just thought it was nuts that *you* wrote it. You. That's what went through my head while I was reading. *Holy shit, Tabitha wrote this*. I'm in awe of you." He says it so matter-of-factly, his voice a low purr. "I couldn't stop picturing you at your laptop in that sexy little baseball hat, pen tucked behind your ear, dreaming up that shit. You're so fucking smart."

Tilting my head a little, I gaze at him with doe eyes. I *know* they're doe eyes because my entire face softens and my whole body gives a blissful, dreamy sigh.

Collin straightens in his seat. "What's that look you're giving me right now?"

I quietly exhale. "What look?" Even *that* comes out sounding breathless and wistful.

His lips curve into a knowing smile. "Don't deny it. You're looking at me like this." He puckers his mouth and flutters his dark, sexy eyelashes. Lowering his voice, he arches one perfect, masculine brow. "You're totally thinking about climbing into my lap right now, aren't you?"

Yes. "No."

He relaxes in his seat and crosses his arms.

God, those arms.

"Pfft. That is *not* how I'm looking at you." My lying eyes go to his lips—his full and soft and pliant lips. Well, I don't know for *sure* that they're soft, but right now there's nothing I'd love more than to find out.

I almost groan out loud at the wayward ideas running rampant through my mind that have nothing to do with enjoying the rest of our four-course meal: Unbuttoning his dress shirt, one button at a time to expose his warm skin. Climbing into his lap. Kissing his neck. Finding out how *happ*y his trail actually is, all the way down to his…

I take a sip of wine to occupy my hands and my tongue, guiltily glancing away.

Collin laughs. "You *dirty*, dirty pervert."

"What?" It's on the tip of my tongue to point out that, as a romance writer, it's practically my job to picture him naked. "If you must know, my thoughts weren't dirty. I was—" I clear my throat so I can lie with a straight face. "I was just…" God, this is torture. "I was just thinking about how *soft* your lips look."

"Soft. My lips?" If a man has ever looked disappointed by a pronouncement, it would be Collin Keller right in this moment. Actually, disappointed doesn't even cover it; the man stares at me, crestfallen. "That's it? You weren't undressing me in your mind?"

"Pretty much."

"Not my muscles or my… cash and prizes?" He raises his eyebrows again. "Soft lips don't sound sexy. Soft lips sound like a snooze-fest."

"Are you *sure* about that?"

The table we're at is square. Small.

Intimate.

Just enough room for the two of us, a few plates, and not much else. Which means with very minimal effort I can prod. "Lean towards me for a second."

I remove the napkin from my lap and brace my elbows on either side of our table. I watch, fascinated, as Collin's hazel eyes run down the length of my neck, over my collarbone, and land on my exposed skin. On the smooth skin of my cleavage.

My breasts.

Lifting myself off the chair gets me closer still, my laser-like focus directed entirely on his mouth. He chooses that moment to slide his tongue over his lips. "Should I pop in a breath mint?"

He sounds so hopeful I almost giggle.

"Shhh." My whisper is centimeters away, so close we're sharing the same breath. Parting my lips ever so slightly, I kiss *just* his bottom lip. Softly, I rest my lips there before teasing him with one small suck. A tender pull. I was right: warm, tender, and so, so soft.

His large hands grab fistfuls of white linen table cloth and clench when I brush my mouth against the irresistible divot above his chiseled chin. Back and forth, back and forth, taking the opportunity to inhale the masculine smell of him. Fresh. Woodsy. Delicious. Virile.

I could have the Big O just from the *smell* of him.

My kiss lands in the corner of his lips. Left side… right side.

His lips part a fraction and holy mother of… it feels so good.

Eyes quivering closed, his body shivers on an inaudible moan. Collin sits utterly still when the flick of my tongue meets his cupid's bow, and I press my entire mouth firmly against his one last time before pulling away.

Mmmmm, mmm, mmm.

Satisfied, I plop back down, settling into my cushy dinner seat. Silently, I calmly lay the napkin across my lap and sink back into my chair, trying to get comfortable. I shoot Collin a long, meaningful look across the table.

He looks about as dazed as I feel.

I grasp my wine glass with unsteady fingers and take a casual sip. "Was that a snooze-fest?"

"*Uh…*" Collin un-fists the tablecloth and smooths out the creases. "I don't know. We should probably do it again to make sure."

I tsk, giving my head a shake. "Let's save some of that mystery for later, shall we?"

"I thought you'd be more like Rachel," he huffs with a pout but gives me a wink. "If I start calling you Rachel, will you start acting like her?"

"In my book, Rachel and Devon had *sex* on the table during one of their dates, remember?" I point out. "No offense, but I think I'd rather sit and eat this sourdough bread." I set down my glass and pull a slice of bread from the loaf. "Wait. Having sex on the table tonight wasn't part of your plan, was it?"

A loud, obnoxious snort fills the room. "No! God no—I was trying to surprise you by doing something romantic. I mean… unless you *want* me to bend you over the table. Shit, sorry, that was…" Chagrined, he blushes and starts over. "You know, this date is the best idea I've ever come up with. And *you're* the one that came up with it. The details were easy to recreate. Wine. Food. Flowers."

Speaking of flowers… "Do you even know what any of these colors mean?"

"The color of the roses? Yeah, I Googled it." Collin takes a drink of Chardonnay. "Red means love, or in this case, passion. Yellow means friendship—or a new beginning." My face reddens as he prattles on. "And peach means closing the deal."

"What about the purple one? That's not in the book." I already know what it means because I had researched their meanings too, but I ask anyway. Just to see if he'll say it.

He hesitates. "Promise you won't freak out?"

I roll my eyes and tease. "Nothing you do would surprise me at this point; you're like a loose cannon. Besides, I'm destined to be a famous writer of smutty romance—it's impossible to shock me."

Hair flip.

He gives a jerky nod, steeling up his courage. Him. This handsome hunk of man, nervous. Imagine that. "Alright, smartass. Lavender means enchantment." His voice deepens. "Tabitha Thompson, I'm without a doubt *enchanted* by you."

Lavender roses also mean *love at first sight*, but I don't say it. Can't say it.

He must know it, too.

Must.

The blush creeps from my cheeks then lower to my chest, over my body, down to my legs. I'm blushing everywhere—from the roots of my hair to the tips of my red painted toenails.

My lips part and I muster a feeble, "Do you Google everything?"

He's not fooled by my casual countenance—not one bit. His beautiful hazel eyes wrinkle at the corners in amusement. "Pretty much."

"Maybe you should stay off the internet," I suggest quietly.

"Maybe I should." He leans back in his dinner seat and crosses his arms, the blue dress shirt stretching and straining over his muscles. "But then again, maybe I shouldn't. I'm always amazed at what I find."

His underlying meaning makes me shiver—and not from the cool air being pumped into the room. Oh boy. Is it hot in here? Waiter! Oh, waiter! Could someone bring me a fan, or a pitcher of water to pour down my pants?

Or maybe that's his line.

"And what did you find when you Googled *me*?"

"Well, Tabitha Thompson—did you know if you google Tabitha Thompson, a whole history of accomplishments pop up? Track and Field scholarship. Summa Cum Laude. A random picture from a Greek Formal you went to." He reaches forward and picks a small baby carrot off his plate, popping it in his mouth. "Sexy dress, by the way."

I look down at my outfit, my eyes hitting my generous cleavage. "This one, or the one I wore to Greek formal?"

"Both." His eyes do a leisurely, appreciative scan of my exposed clavicle and the swell of my breasts.

I stab blindly at the plate in front of me with my fork, spearing a hunk of seafood and stuffing it in my mouth so I don't have to reply.

Classy, right?

I swallow and say, "How did you know these were

my favorite foods?"

"Easy." Collin smiles. "Your brother through my sister. And the best part is, they're my favorite foods, too."

We continue eating in silence, giving each other furtive glances over wine and steak and lobster. When dessert comes—crème brûlée and banana cream pie, more of my favorites—we share, wordlessly passing the plates and spoons back and forth between us like we've been dating for years.

Heaven. Every mouthwatering bite. Every delicious time our eyes meet.

We sip wine, falling into easy conversation. So easy. Natural. Relaxed. Collin grabs my hand and finds my knee under the table with his other, giving my smooth skin slow, gentle strokes until I'm biting my lip and looking away.

Then we're leaning into each other across the tiny table, our knees touching, our lips pressing together. My eyes flutter closed as Collin's hand finds my inner thigh, the other finding the nape of my neck, pulling me in closer. Sweetly. Hungrily.

Aroused.

Our mouths part and our tongues touch, exploring deliberately. An unhurried pleasure that sends a shockwave of desire between my legs and surging through my body.

This isn't just a kiss; this is an unspoken invitation for something more. More meaningful. Full of surrender.

I will worship you, the kiss whispers.

I will be good to you, the kiss promises.

It doesn't last long. Collin pulls away first, resting his forehead against mine, stroking the underside of my jaw with his thumb.

He's breathing hard.

I'm breathing hard.

"Tabitha." His voice is a low, gravelly plead. "Tabitha, come home with me."

I will worship you...

I will be good to you...

I know I shouldn't. I know it's too soon to be intimate. But I know if I don't...

I'll regret it.

I give a barely perceivable nod. "Yes."

Yes.

***B**lare Wellborn did not sleep around. Didn't do one-night stands. Didn't sleep with men on the first date. But as she looked across the table at him, the only sensible thought running through her mind was... nothing. There were no sensible thoughts, only need and want and desperation. For him. For Collin Adam.*

He slid his hand across her knee. "Blare, come home with me." All she could do was nod, the words lost in her throat. When he got her home she would see to it that he worshipped the column of the smooth skin there—her favorite spot to be kissed.

"You want me to come home with you? I want to, but... I barely know you. We've only known each other, what—three weeks?"

He leans in and presses a kiss to her chin. "Blare Wellborn, I am enchanted by you." With those seven words, all her fears melted away...

Greyson: *What's going on? Hello! I haven't heard from you in days…*

Tabitha: *Sorry! I'm sorry. Work has been so busy.*

Greyson: *Busy? I hate when people say that. Busy is just an excuse.*

Tabitha: *You're right—I haven't been THAT busy, but I do have a confession to make.*

Greyson: *A confession?! I like the sound of that!*

Tabitha: *The truth is, I've been spending some time with your, um.*

Greyson: *My, um… what?*

Tabitha: *I've been spending time with Collin. Your brother.*

Greyson: *WHAT? Since when? What kind of time?! How! What? LOL. I mean—WOW! In a good way!!!!!!!*

Tabitha: *Phew. I was kind of worried.*

Greyson: *Are you kidding me? You're amazing. He's awesome (most of the time)! My second and third favorite people. Cal is obviously my FIRST favorite… dating! Love it.*

Tabitha: *Not dating, just thinking about it?*

Greyson: *So where are you right now? What are you doing tonight?*

Tabitha: *We just went to dinner and now we're… uh… heading to his condo?*

Greyson: *RIGHT NOW???? This very second??? Is he there with you?*

Tabitha: *Yes? Is that bad? I'm so nervous my hands are shaking.*

Greyson: *Tabitha Elizabeth Thompson, you'd better be "dating" if you're HEADED TO HIS CONDO at eleven o'clock on a Saturday night!!!! Do I need to Mom lecture you about "safety"? cough cough*

Tabitha: *Oh god, please don't.*

Greyson: *I'm not ready for nieces and nephews yet, just so you know. Even if he is 26. Nevermind—I'll take a niece…*

Tabitha: *NO. Just no!*

Greyson: *Alright, I'll stop, but only on one condition: you tell me everything later. Well, not EVERYTHING…*

Tabitha: *It's a deal. <3 you*
Greyson: *<3*

11

Collin

We don't go through the pretense of wanting after-dinner drinks when we arrive at my condo, don't make small talk in my living room, don't loiter in the kitchen.

I bypass a tour entirely, assuming she took one during my housewarming party, and lead her by the hand up the stairs to the master bedroom. I give it a squeeze when I push open the double doors, and she steps over the threshold first, walking to the bed, sitting, and crossing her legs.

Flushed, she rests back, bracing herself up by the elbows on my soft mattress, and I stroll in after her, flipping on a newly acquired table lamp from Target. I give my shirt collar a tug, loosening the top button and leisurely sliding it through the hole. One. Two. Two buttons undone.

Those hypnotic blue eyes never leave my face.

Three buttons.

The pads of Tabitha's fingertips lightly caress my white duvet cover, stroking it softly. "Are these the crisp, clean sheets that Greyson said would be nice to roll around on that day I found you shopping?"

"Hell yeah." A chuckle escapes my throat.

She swallows and licks those juicy lips. "Good choice."

My fingers pull a fourth button unfastened. Five. "You impressed? I got me a new wine bottle opener, too."

"Oh, fancy." Her voice is throaty and breathless.

"You like the sheets, Tabitha?"

"Oh *yeah*."

Six.

"You should see yourself. Hair all over, skin all hot. I couldn't be more turned on. You're so fucking sexy."

Her hooded eyes leave my face to rake me up and down, searing, as I pluck button number seven free. "So are you."

"You know what would make us even sexier?"

Eight.

"What?" she says in the barest hint of a whisper.

Her legs part voluntarily when I kneel… go down on bended knee… unbuckle the thin straps on her high-heeled shoes, each one the same color as her flesh and sexy as shit. I remove them both and kiss the top of her foot before tossing both heels off to the side. They hit the closet door with a loud thud. I ignore them, running my palms up her silky thighs, letting them roam up and under the skirt of her dress, parting the seam in the process.

I watch, transfixed, as Tabitha's eyes flutter shut, losing herself in the feel of my hands gliding across her skin.

Still on my knees, I inch forward to settle myself between her legs and wrap my arms around her waist. I trail kisses along her collarbone, the glowing skin where her shoulder and neck meet.

Tabitha tips her head back to give my greedy-as-fuck lips access, her long blonde hair falling to the comforter, cascading like a waterfall. Stunning. I take a few strands, rubbing them between two fingers, then lift them to my nose.

"Your hair smells amazing." I drop the locks and my lips speak into the hollow of her neck. "You smell like I want to do *this*."

This is my tongue trailing the length of her collarbone.

Tabitha moans, stiffening slightly.

"What are we doing, Collin? What are we doing," she pants. "This isn't me. I don't d-do one-night stands." She releases another moan when my tongue licks the hollow between her breasts. "I'm a... *mmm*... relationship kind of girl."

"So am I," I respond dumbly, my mouth nipping her bare skin, hands pushing aside the soft fabric of her dress, lips grazing her bare shoulder.

Tabitha gives her head a little shake.

"I would never bring this up, but... *oh god, that feels good*... we're stuck with each other no matter what. Cal and Grey are going to end up married and... *mmmm*... we're going to be in each other's lives whether... *your tongue is amazing*... or not."

Tabitha threads her fingers through my hair, roughly

raking her nails along my scalp. Her back is arched with pleasure, and my large hands move up and down her spine, kneading. I wet the pulse in her neck with my tongue, too. "Good. I want you to be stuck with me. You're so goddamn sexy."

I wonder if she knows what a turn-on her brain is, her *mind*.

No lie.

"What will our parents say?" she asks with bated breath into my hair as my fingers splay across her middle, enjoying the feel of her silky dress beneath my fingers. But not for long: she needs to be naked. "All their kids dating each other. Collin, it's not normal."

"Who gives a shit? I don't." My mouth finds purchase on the swells of her breasts and my fingers deftly work the belt on her dress. Swiftly. *Done*. "You're beautiful."

Her fingers continue their savage plunge through my—

"I love your thick hair."

I'm close to purring like a goddamn jungle cat when she massages my scalp. "I love your hands."

"I love *your* hands."

These hands are going to make her feel even better. I nuzzle her cleavage again with my nose and inhale the musk of her perfume.

"I fucking love your boobs." I palm one through her dress. "Definitely love these boobs."

Tabitha tips her head back and laughs through a gasp. "Take off your shirt."

Oh, now she's giving orders? "Take off your dress."

But I stand to pull the last few pearl buttons through their holes. She stops me.

"Wait, let me do it."

I watch, mesmerized, as her nimble fingers fly down the seam of my shirt. She spreads her hands on my bare chest when she succeeds in releasing the remaining button. Her palms span flat over my washboard abs.

Her breath hitches in wonderment. "I was right."

"About?"

"This is one of the *happiest* trails I've ever seen." Still sitting on the edge of my bed, the tip of her finger leisurely traces the narrow path of hair that runs from my belly button, and disappears into the waistband of my pants.

I swallow. "When… when were you thinking about my happy trail?" She stands, both palms traveling flat over my abs, roaming the length of my stomach, pecs, and up, over my shoulders. Unhurriedly, they descend again towards my belt buckle in such a slow, deliberate pace it almost makes my leg twitch with urgency.

Like a dog in heat.

"When was I thinking about all *this*? *Hmm…*" Tabitha hums. The sound of metal coming unfastened, leather sliding, and a thud on the ground are the only sounds filling the air. "The minute I found out you *weren't* Greyson's new boyfriend, my mind went there. And stayed there."

Her talented fingers work the fly of my pants, then the zipper.

Jesus.

I bite my lip and deeply inhale towards the ceiling, count to… to… *shit yes…* to control my breathing as my large body begins to vibrate, strumming high with eagerness.

Tabitha's fingers skim my waistband, tormenting.

Grasping my black slacks, she *finally* fucking pushes them down my hips. I step out of the legs, kicking them aside like a Neanderthal so they land in a heap near her shoes, out of the way. It wouldn't be cool to trip on that shit once we're frantically stumbling around bare-ass naked.

And we will be naked *soon*.

Guaranteed.

She teases, stroking me with a feather-light touch. "You really do have the best hands," I damn near whimper. It sounds like I'm whining as goosebumps cover my skin.

Fucking goosebumps—and she hasn't even stroked my cock yet.

"That's what *all* the boys say." She giggles then at my sullen expression. "What? I've always wanted to use that line out loud."

"Maybe you should use it in your next book."

"Maybe I should."

Impatiently, I begin working the sash on her dress, yanking it free and letting it limply fall to the side. My fingers, of their own accord, pursue her skin like a heat-seeking missile. Tabitha bites her lower lip when I push her dress all the way open, permitting the pads of my hands to roam her body, the flat planes of her stomach, the plump breasts pressed together by a sheer, nearly transparent push-up bra.

Barely there, flesh-toned G-string.

If I didn't know any better, I'd think… "Were you *planning* on getting naked tonight?"

With a single shrug, off comes the dress. It cascades to the floor. "You'll never know, will you? And I'll never tell."

Tabitha Thompson, you secretive little sneak.

My hands reach out, grab on, and toss her on the waiting bed.

It wants to get laid, too.

Tabitha

When our clothes fall to the carpet and the pile of fabric is discarded, I waste no time scooting to the center of Collin's bed in my bra and panties. It's been who knows how many months since anyone has touched me intimately, and my body is alive with *everything* for Collin.

He follows on all fours, crawling towards me from the foot of the bed, kissing his way up my leg, starting at my ankles, dusting kisses on the insides of my thighs that leave me trembling almost uncontrollably.

I spread my legs desperately, affording him easier access to all my sensitive spots, because let's face it—it feels ah-freaking-mazing and my inner slut has apparently been unleashed.

I want it so bad.

I do everything but thrash my head around on the pillow as Collin's mouth grazes my stomach at the same time his forefinger hooks itself under the seam of my sheer underwear. The rude asshole teases with a tug, releasing the elastic with a snap and leaves them on.

I touch his shoulders, urging him upward till he stops, his mouth latching onto my nipple through my bra, sucking and sucking and swirling his tongue until the mesh is soaked through.

"Oh *j-jesus* that f-feels…" Yeah. *That* good.

When our mouths finally meet, we're tortured and aroused at the same time, noisily groaning our relief. His large, hard body is smooth and firm, and I can feel every inch of him.

Every *solid* inch.

He's so hard.

His dick is so *hard*.

It feels s-so… so… *oh god…*

But I'm not relieved—not *nearly*—and won't be until he gives me what we both want. Lord, listen to me, using words I've written in my own books—chapter seven, as a matter of fact.

Thank god I didn't blurt it out loud. Then again, as I get to know him better, it would probably turn him on hearing me talk all smutty and dirty.

His skin is sweaty and warm and I want to lick him all over.

I want him to lick *me* all over. All. Over.

And then, as if reading my mind… he does.

Yes! Shit *yes*.

"Do you like that, baby?" he murmurs as his hot lips follow a path from my stomach to my clavicle. Normally I can't stand tallking during sex—and I can't stand the word *baby*—but coming from Collin? He can call me anything he wants. I am putty in his large, capable hands.

My overactive imagination kicks into overdrive as the sound of our panting and kissing fills the air. I do nothing but lie like a limp rag doll beneath him, raising my arms above my head and grabbing hold of the fluffy pillow.

"I knew it was you the moment I saw you." His praises reach my soul, even as his mammoth hands worship my breasts. "You're all I think about. Jesus, Tabitha, stop rocking your hips like that."

But I don't stop. I release the pillow, reaching my hands between our bodies to stroke him up and down through his boxer briefs. He's long and ready and throbbing. "Why are we still wearing fucking clothes? Take these off."

The wait is unbearable.

Agonizing.

I'm begging now. "Please, Collin, take them off."

"You don't have to fucking tell me twice." He rolls off me to swiftly strip himself bare, and I do the same, fumbling to unclasp my bra and peel off my underwear, dropping them to the floor.

"I don't know if I can wait." Collin licks my ear lobe as he settles himself between my thighs, stiff in all the right places. I moan my appreciation—loudly—into the hollow of his neck when he rotates his pelvis, grinding into me, and press a kiss to his Adam's apple. "I'm gonna make you come so hard.""

I want more.

He gives it to me.

Yes... *Yes,* Collin. *More.*

12

Collin

A distraction: that's what she's been for the past several weeks. I wanted her blonde, beautiful, and beneath me.

And now she's here.

Her neck thrown back as my mouth eagerly imprints the smooth, bare skin of her shoulder, Tabitha's golden hair spills across my pillow. I brush the hair out of her face, cupping her jawline with my palm.

My thumb strokes her bottom lip and I lower my chin until our lips meld together. Brush back and forth. Once. Twice.

I savor the feel of our naked bodies pressed together, impatient to feel her around my hardened cock, the pulsing between my legs almost *un*-fucking-*bearable,* wanting to dig in deep.

I don't want to rush her, but—

"Condom, now. Collin, Collin," she chants my name. "Enough playing around. I need it *now*."

I give it to her then, sliding in and nailing her slow and fast and… *motherfucker*… Soft and hard and… *fuck, Tabitha, right fucking there*… Slick with sweat, the air thick with urgency, we move in sync, whispering. Demanding. Coaxing.

Gasping.

The fucking moaning never ends.

"Yes… oh, mmm, *God*, Collin… Collin… *Uh! Oh god…*"

"…Hold on tight to the headboard, baby... Fuck me, Tabitha, just like that…"

"…Right there… p-please don't stop, *don't stop, don't... stop…*"

We're raw. We're tender.

We're a walking, talking cliché.

Fuck. *Yeah.*

Tabitha

We settle into a pattern after our night together—meeting at Blooming Grounds during the work week; he works and I write. Laughing, talking. Dinners. Hiking.

Movies at his place.

Our feelings for each other grow; we ache.

We *burn*.

We hold hands, talk, kiss constantly. Cuddle.

Touch.

And have sex. Lots and lots of hot, incredible sex.

We make love, too.

Collin Keller is everything I've ever wanted—everything I've only fantasized about in writing.

Blare watched Adam from across the bedroom as he pulled off his shirt, stalked over, and pulled back the covers on his side of her bed. Sliding in, he reached over, trailing a hand down her bare stomach. "Tired?" he asked, kissing her shoulder.

"Yes and no," she said, stretching like a feline alley cat, satisfied and content. "It was a long day." Blare might have worked for her parents during the day, but she

had a side project she worked on at night. Moonlighting as an artist was taking its toll.

Adam went further down her body, disappearing under the covers. "Sweetie, don't you think it's time to tell someone besides me?" His voice was tentative and unsure. He'd suggested it before, but... "I'm not ready. Give me time."

"When will it be time, Blare? It's been over a year."

Blare stiffened under his inquisition, but softened immediately when his fingers... did that thing... right... there...in that *spot... "Yes. I know. I will, but I have to be the one to tell, okay? Promise you won't say anything."*

He kissed her neck. Nipped at her breasts. Licked in that spot that drove her absolutely wild.

"Baby, I promise." Adam kissed her abs. Her belly button. "You can trust me. I won't tell a soul...."

Blare lost herself in him then as he worshiped her body. Loving him.

Trusting him...

13

Collin

"Greyson tells me you've been spending shit tons of time with my sister. That's a big change from her avoiding you at your party." That's something I've always respected about Cal since he started dating Greyson; he doesn't fuck around. When he wants to know something, he asks—he doesn't beat around the bush, and he's not passive aggressive.

But that doesn't mean I have to give him a full shakedown of my personal business.

I glance over my shoulder in the direction of the restrooms, where the girls have disappeared to. We're at a bar in Calumet, the city where Cal attends an Ivy League university, and coordinated the trip for a weekend Greyson happened to be staying with him.

Win-win for all of us.

For Tabitha and me, it was like killing two birds with one stone, getting to visit them both at once. It's also the first time our siblings will see us acting like an actual couple.

"Dude. Are you listening to me?" Cal prods me in the ribs.

"We're having fun."

Lot of sex. *Lots* of fun.

"We're having fun?" He snorts, resting his elbows on the counter in the bar we're sitting in. "Humor me and define *fun*, would you, because you say *fun* and all I hear is *I'm banging your sister*."

Cal uses air quotes when he sarcastically intones the word fun.

He's perceptive. Calculating. And clearly not amused.

I look him in the eye, tapping the bottom of the beer bottle in my hand against the counter. "Without getting into detail, Tabitha and I are friends—"

"It better not be friends with fucking benefits."

"Would you let me finish?" Okay, initially I assumed he was going to be cool with me dating his sister, but now I'm not so sure. I tread lightly, choosing my next words carefully. Don't get me wrong—Cal is cool guy and he's perfect for Greyson, but he's also built like a tank, has about thirty pounds on me, and I've literally watched him suckerpunch a guy between the eyes during a rugby match. So yeah. Pissing him off is not on the itinerary.

"Tabitha and I are friends. I'm not *just* physically attracted to her; I respect the shit out of her. Do you even know how amazing she is?" I take a swig of beer. "The minute I saw her, I just kn—why the fuck are you staring at me like that? Am I starting to sound like a goddamn pansy?"

Cal rolls his eyes. "The minute you saw her at your housewarming party?"

"No, man, the minute I saw her hiding behind a rack of chairs at Target, working herself up into a tizzy, wearing that cute pink hat. So fucking adorable." I chuckle when Cal looks back at me, his brows scrunched into a confused scowl.

"My sister is not adorable. She overreacts to *everything* and is a giant pain in the…" He stops short when I cock an eyebrow.

He shakes his head, regathering his thoughts. "Look, I'm not going to start an argument with you. All I'm saying is you better not be playing around. She's dated enough assholes; she doesn't need to date another one."

"Have you ever *met* your sister? Pretty sure she'd have my balls in a vise if I screwed her over." Cal nods in agreement. I swallow what's left in my beer bottle before waxing poetic. "So sweet I can barely stand it. Last night she surprised me with a—"

"Keller, *stop*." My sister's boyfriend curls his lips, disgusted. "You've obviously never seen her throw a hissy fit about having to chop fire wood on the weekends at our parents' house."

I scoff, unimpressed. "*Puh-lease*. You think that's bad? I'll counter a wood-chopping hissy fit and raise you one *you've obviously never seen Greyson stuff eighteen marshmallows in her mouth at one time*. Ask her to play Chubby Bunny with you once."

Cal's blue eyes widen. "Seriously? Eighteen marshmallows? Dude, what the fuck."

"Yes, seriously. It's a game they used to play at sleep-away camp. Then she'd come home and play it with her friends. It's freakishly disturbing." I grimace at the memory of my dainty, blonde-haired and bright-eyed little sister—my parents' pride and joy—cramming white puff after white puff of fluffy marshmallow into her mouth as a teenager.

Like a boss.

My sister's boyfriend snickers. "Well, being able to fit large objects in her mouth is a skill that comes in handy for us both—where can I send my thank-you letter?"

"Ha ha, *real* funny, asshole."

Cal's booming laughter echoes loudly, sounding unpracticed and rusty as the girls re-approach, Greyson taking the lead with Tabitha nipping at her heels.

She eyes us skeptically.

"What are you two laughing at?" Greyson asks, automatically shimmying up to Cal, her body contouring to his—like two puzzle pieces that were made to fit together. Her arm slips around his waist while narrowing those light hazel eyes at me.

My sister unattractively purses her lips.

"What? What did *I* do?" I ask. "What's with the stink-eye?"

Those slits of hazel get thinner. "What did you tell him?"

I immediately grab a square white cocktail napkin from the center of the table, wad it up, and shove it in my mouth. "Chubby bunny."

"Oh my god!" Greyson laughs and smacks me in the arm. Hard. "You shithead!"

I wad up another one. It joins the first. "Chubby.

Bunny."

"Stop it, Collin, or you'll choke. I don't want to have to call Mom and Dad from the hospital because you're jamming napkins down your throat."

"Hey, I was forced into it—we were comparing bratty sister stories." My voice is muffled around the two napkins packed in my mouth. A white corner sticks out from between my lips as I continue. "He didn't leave me any choice."

I can't tell by Tabitha's neutral expression if she's amused or appalled by my childish antics.

My sister grabs a cocktail napkin, balls it up in her fist, and throws it at me, laughing. "On second thought, here. Shove this one in your face, too. Maybe it'll shut you up." Greyson turns to Tabitha and rolls her eyes. "Honestly, I don't know what you see in him, and now I have to question your taste in men. For a grown man, sometimes he is *so* immature."

Tabitha giggles.

Cal glances back and forth between his sister and me. "Wait. For real, you're seeing each other? I thought you were full of shit before."

"No. Why would you think I was full of shit?"

He glances at his sister. "I mean, I love you, Tabby, so no offense—I'm just not used to seeing you dating anyone. I was already in college when you were dating that douchebag baseball player, and even *I* knew he didn't deserve you."

I move closer to Tabitha, pull her in, and relax my hand on her hip. "Damn right he didn't deserve her," I add, even though I have no idea what baseball player he's talking about. I make a mental note to ask about it later. "Your sister is incredible."

"I *know* that, Collin. I'm just saying she's dated some real dickshitters."

"Not on purpose," Tabitha points out, resting her head on my shoulder. I give her a squeeze. "Remember Bryan Rickman? *He* wasn't completely horrible."

Cal laughs. "Correct me if I'm wrong, but didn't you date him in *ninth* grade?"

"What's your point?"

"That doesn't count. You were fourteen."

She narrows her bright blue eyes. "How do you even remember all this?"

Cal blushes, the gash on his face appearing even more severe. Chagrined, he mutters, "I may or may not have read your diary." Tabitha hauls off and whacks him with her purse. "Ouch! I said I *may* have! Jeez! There's no tangible proof that I actually did."

"Okay, break it up you two," Greyson referees, stepping in. "Go to your rooms."

But Cal is on a roll and brings the conversation full circle. "Really though, I'm just curious—how *did* you end up hooking up in the first place?" He grimaces. "I didn't mean hooking up. I meant *talking*."

"Dating?" Tabitha clears her throat. "Well, coincidentally, we ran into each other one afternoon doing out-of-office work stuff. Sometimes I take everything to a coffee shop, sit with my laptop, and drink coffee."

I agree. "Same. And that's what we were doing when we bumped into each other before the housewarming—"

"He scared the crap out of me—" Tabitha interrupts.

"She had the most adorable panic attack and spilled coffee all over herself. All over her white shirt. I was hoping it would turn into a wet tee-shirt contest—"

"Shut up, you were making me nervous!"

"I was making *you* nervous? *Pretty* sure it was the other way around."

"Oh my god, you are so sweet." She pecks my cheek, excited, then speaks to her brother. "So he's just standing there staring, right, which was weirding me out. I end up knocking everything off the table, including the proof of my book—"

"It just lands under the table," I add with a knowing smirk.

Tabitha throws her arms in the air. "And what does he do? Nothing! Doesn't say a word about it, the shithead."

We entertain Greyson and Cal, volleying barbs.

"What was I supposed to do? I had to get your attention somehow. Pocketing the book you wrote was the best way to do it…"

"Well, you didn't have to steal it and hold it hostage so I'd go out with you." She slaps my arm playfully, squeezing my bicep in the process. I flex. "It was so rude. He used it to blackmail me into going on our first date."

"Puh-*lease*, don't even act like you were going to say no—"

"I was going to say no! You were so annoying." She punctuates this pronouncement with a kiss to my jawline before enthusiastically prattling on. "He was purposely trying to embarrass me. He even read out loud from chapter ten when we met up. I finally agreed to meet him because I *really* needed it back."

Lost in our own stream of babbling nonsense, neither of us realizes why Calvin and Greyson are staring at us, slack-jawed.

Wait.

Why the fuck *are* they staring at us like that?

Was it something we said? Did we….

Oh shit.

Oh. Fucking. *Shit*.

I squeeze Tabitha's waist, prodding her to stop talking. In her excitement, she doesn't even realize we blurted out her secret. That with her rambling, she's giving away her secret, too.

Cal holds his palm up to stop us. "Back up. Did you guys just say the book she wrote? What book? Who wrote it?"

I feign ignorance. "Did we say that?"

"Yes, jackhole, you did." He looks point blank at his sister, a dark cloud descending on his expression. "Tabby, did you write a *novel*?"

"Uh…" She stands frozen, rooted to the floor, stunned. "Oh my god. I told, didn't I? Collin, please tell me I didn't just…"

Silence.

Followed by the inevitable.

Tabitha pulls away, unfolding herself from my body. I try to stop her by grabbing her upper arm, but she surprises me by giving me a shove so hard I stumble back a few steps. "Tabitha, it just slipped out. Babe, calm down—"

"Just slipped out! Just slipped out? Oh my god, I was going on and on about it! I'm such an *idiot*. An idiot!" She throws her arms in the air, defeated, and turns to confront me, poking me in the chest with the tip of an index finger, ignoring her brother and my sister. Angry. Frustrated. "One year, Collin. *One*. *Year*. Twelve months. Fifty-two weeks. That's how long I've kept my novel a secret." She stomps away, huffing and muttering to herself before stomping back. "Everyone is going to hate me for lying! How am I going to look my parents in the eye, and see my grandma on the weekend after they find out? They're going to think I'm a... a... Collin, I just told everyone the secret I've been keeping from them for an entire year!"

"Well, not *every*one. Mom and Dad aren't here," her brother interjects, trying to be helpful.

"Shut *up*, Calvin. This is between me and Collin," Tabitha admonishes with a loud shriek. Okay, maybe it's not a shriek, exactly, but it's definitely a cross between a scream and a whine.

Whoa, nelly, calm down.

She seriously needs to chill.

I'm not a *complete* idiot, so I compress my mouth shut, determined to power through her tirade.

"This was my well-guarded secret. How could I have been so stupid? What was I thinking! God, why didn't I just tell you *no* when you asked me out the first time? This never would have happened. I'm such an idiot."

Wait. Is she blaming *me*?

"Tab, please. Calm down, sweetie, be reasonable. This is a *good* thing, can't you see it? I'm sorry, but maybe your brother knowing—"

"No. Forget it, Collin. This isn't for you to decide. You don't get to tell me to calm down." She grabs her purse off the table.

"Tabitha, stop. Where the hell are you going?"

"I need time to think about what I'm gonna do. Alone."

Except, we're in a college town, staying with her

brother for Christ's sake, not back home where she can hitch a cab and go back to her place.

"Take me back to your apartment, Cal. I can't sit in a car with him for three whole hours right now. Not just yet." Tabitha drags her brother towards the door by the upper arm. "I just have to get out of here. Think."

He's powerless to fight her, instead launching an inquisition.

"What novel?" I hear Cal asks as he's physically being led away. "Did you write a book, Tabby? Will someone please tell me what's going on?"

"No."

She's so angry. At herself. At me.

Irrational.

From beside me, my sister places a caring hand gently on my forearm, reminding me of her presence. "So, I take it Tabitha wrote a novel and didn't want to tell anyone?"

My head gives a jerky nod. "Yeah."

"Wow." Pause. "That is so... *cool*."

"Yeah."

"Why would she keep it a secret?"

My broad shoulders shrug feebly. "Because it's romance. The slutty kind."

"Wow," Greyson repeats. "That is so... *awesome*."

Tell me about it.

Grey rests her palm on my shoulder and gives it a squeeze. "This will blow over. You'll see." My sister's words are quiet and slightly skeptical.

"Yeah."

But even I don't believe it.

Collin: *Tabitha, would you please answer my calls? You barely spoke on the car ride home and you're not responding to my texts. We need to talk.*

Collin: *Please. I'm so fucking sorry they found out that way, but it was bound to come out eventually.*

Collin: *Greyson told me that your brother told your parents. What did they say? Please call me back.*

Collin: *Did you get the roses I sent to your office? I didn't want to be cheesy and I know you're pissed, but the red, yellow, lavender, and peach roses say everything—please, Tabitha. Let me tell you in person how I feel about you. Please.*

Tabitha's Notes for Book THREE, title to be determined. Titles I'm considering: THE BETRAYAL. Back cover blurb: Tarran felt betrayed by the world. By the one man she loved. Handsome and clever, the quick-witted devil had become her downfall. Because of him, the walls she'd so carefully erected around herself didn't just fall; they imploded...

14

Tabitha

"Honey, can I come in?" A few short knocks at my office door interrupt my thoughts, and quickly, I close the expanded document on my laptop screen when my dad sticks his head in.

Ironically, building up walls has become my specialty lately.

"Sure, Dad. Of course."

It's his company and his building; the man hardly needs permission.

His distinguished salt-and-pepper gray hair appears in the doorway, leading the way inside my office, the permanent smile he's never without pasted across his face. Around his eyes, weathered from the elements and years of working outdoors, are well-earned wrinkles and laugh lines.

We get our humor from him, Cal and I.

"Come in. Want to sit?" I indicate a spare chair in the corner.

Plopping himself unceremoniously in the chair that has been around this office longer than I've been alive, my father, Hodge Thompson, stretches, crosses his arms, and looks around.

"I haven't been in here for quite a while." He inches forward, plucking a framed photograph of me and my college roommate Savannah off my mahogany desk, studies it wordlessly, then sets it back in its place. "Your mom will be joining us shortly."

My mom and dad sitting in here together?

Oh crap, this can only mean one thing: an ambush.

I give a stiff laugh. "Is this an intervention?"

He raises a gray brow. "Why, do you need one?"

"Good one, Dad." I feign ignorance, forcing out a fake laugh. "Are the two of you taking me to lunch or something?"

He raises his other eyebrow and gives me "the look." You know the one your parents give you when *they* know *you* know *they* think you're full of shit.

Did that even make sense? For an author, I can't even string a few words together today.

Wait. Did I just call myself an author?

Crap. I did, didn't I?

I've never had that thought before—that I'm an author. A writer. And now I can't help but wonder why it suddenly crossed my mind, now of all times, with my parents about to lecture me about... who knows what.

Nope, that's a lie. I know exactly what they're going

to lecture me about, thanks to Collin and my loud-mouth brother.

My writing. My book.

My *novel*.

I slump down in my desk chair a little, swiveling towards the window to avoid my mother's gaze when she swoops into the room, sophisticated, blonde haired, and blue eyed.

"Sorry I'm late! Did I miss anything?" She bends and kisses my dad on the top of his head, then lowers herself into the chair beside him, dropping her purse on the floor. Her hands go to her hair, and she fluffs. "Ugh, how gorgeous is it outside? Too bad we're stuck inside."

Mom, who does the accounting for the company, looks pointedly in my direction. "Take a break, both of you, and make some time to sit outside for a few. Get some fresh air."

I grab the nearest pencil and anxiously tap it on the surface of my desk. "I'll try." I scan their faces. "So..?"

My dad starts, and, having no patience for bullshit, cuts right to the chase. "So. You wrote a book."

He states it as a fact, not as a question.

Denying it would be futile, so I nod. "But it didn't interfere with my work, I swear. I didn't use company time to write, and I used my own laptop."

My mom instantly looks deflated. "Honey, that's not what he meant." She reaches towards the desk and nabs the pencil from my nervous hands. "We want to know why you didn't tell us."

Because.

Because.

I have a million reasons why, but when I open my

mouth to give them, no words spill out. Then I say, "What did Calvin tell you?"

Dad shakes his head, shrugging his broad shoulders. "Nothing. Just that you wrote a book. And that no one knew about it."

"It's a novel, actually," I blurt out, unable to stop myself, and then I regret it when they both raise their eyebrows in surprise. "Sorry."

Dad clears his throat. "He also said you've been seeing the Keller boy." Unable to resist, I roll my eyes at that. The Keller boy. "He's the one you were with when you spilled the proverbial beans, I assume?"

Only my dad would use air quotes when he said 'proverbial beans,' like it was a *thing*.

"*Sort of* seeing him. Yes."

My mom, who can't resist meddling in my love life, chooses her next words carefully. "Honey, why are you taking this whole thing out on this nice young man? Cal says you walked out on him. How is any of this his fault?"

Because I'm stubborn and willful and embarrassed. But of course, I don't say any of this. Instead, I shrug, gazing out my office window for the answers.

"Tabitha." My mother's voice holds a sharp edge. "Did you hear what I said?"

God, I hate it when she talks to me like this, like I'm a child. I feel my chin start to wobble a little when I open my mouth to say, "Why did I take it out on Collin? Because it was easier to get mad at him rather than myself. Because I knew I was wrong. I needed someone to blame and he was there."

Mom leans back in her seat and waits for me to continue.

"God, I acted so juvenile." A tear slips down my cheek, and I swipe at it with my shirtsleeve, refusing to stare into the faces of my disappointed parents. "He's so great, Mom. I hope... I hope you get the chance to meet him."

"If he's anything like his sister, I'm sure we're going to love him."

"He is. You will."

Silence fills the room then, and when my dad doesn't continue where my mom left off, she sniffs impatiently. "Your father and I aren't here to talk about your relationship, although we were concerned about it when we heard." She shoots a pointed look at my dad, to get him on board with the discussion. "The real reason we wanted to sit you down was to tell you that we're *proud* of you, honey. Of course we were shocked! But not for the reason you'd think. Tabitha, sweetie, you wrote a novel!"

"God damn right my girl did!" my dad booms, accompanying his decree with a bang of his fist to my desktop. "My daughter wrote a book. A goddamn book!"

"Hodge," my mom scolds him for cursing, and rolls her eyes impatiently. "Anyway. The thing we're disappointed in, is that you were afraid to tell us. The thought that you kept that *secret* from your father and me for a year makes me... so *sad* for you, sweetie. It breaks my heart that you'd even think we wouldn't support you."

"I..." I look down at my folded hands, clasped together on my desk. "I know you depend on me. I went to college for this, for freaking construction. Do you know how many women were in my classes? Hardly any. Then I had to go to an Ivy League school. Who does that? Why didn't I just go to State, for crying out loud?" I'm on a roll now that the floodgates have opened. Cathartic, I forage on, mindless of the consequences my words might have. "This is the only job I've ever had since I was in middle school, working in the office—why would I leave to be a writer? Talk about a bad decision."

"Honey, your dad and I—"

"And then there's Cal," I blurt out. "He's counting on me to be here when you and Dad retire, which is when? Eight more years? Seven? Then what? He'll hardly be qualified to take over by himself. I'm not either, but at least I have a few more years of management under my belt."

My parents glance at each other, worried that I've lost my damn mind, then back at me. "Tabitha Elizabeth, haven't we always told you, you can be anything you want to be?"

Where is Mom going with this? "Well... *yes*."

"Then why are you working here?"

My head snaps up. "What?"

What does that even mean?

"If you want to be a writer, why are you working here?"

"I just told you. Weren't you listening?" My voice is meek. Weak. Pitiful.

For a strong, independent woman, I sound *pitiful*.

I suck.

"You do not suck, sweetie."

Oh shit, did I say that out loud?

"There you go again. Do you always mutter to yourself?" my dad asks. "I hope you don't do that around our clients." He chuckles. "It's bad for business."

My mom smacks him in the arm. "*Hodge*."

"What your mom and I are trying to tell you is we want you to follow your dreams. We never meant for you to be imprisoned here."

"Dad, that's not it at all!"

He ignores me. "If you need to stay working here while you get on your feet—until your books take off and you can earn a living—then you're welcome to stay. If you want to take some time off, we'll help you do that."

"Help me do... what?"

"Well, you're twenty-four years old, but if you want to move back home to save money—"

Ew.

"I am not moving back in with you. No offense, guys."

"We're just giving you options. You're not stuck here. I know you've always thought you were responsible for holding down the fort until your brother was old enough to take on more responsibility, but give me some credit. That's what Dale and Roger are for."

Dale and Roger are my dad's Vice President of Operations and General Manager.

"But... they're not family. I thought you wanted this to remain a family business."

"Sweetie," my mom puts in sharply. "Now you're just being ridiculous. Maybe that would have been possible twenty years ago, but times are changing." She pats my dad on the hand. "Do you hear your daughter, Hodge? She thinks we're not with the times."

They both laugh. "I bet she doesn't think we know all about them Timber and the Tweeter Apps. Please, we're down with that."

My mom makes a gesture with her hands that looks

surprisingly thug. Gangster even.

"Please stop throwing hands signs," I plead.

She does it again.

"Don't do that. Please stop."

Mom laughs. "Greyson showed me that Bumble site last time Cal brought her home. You should see some of the young hunks online these days."

"It's an app mom, not a website."

She waves her hand in the air. "Same thing."

No, it's not the same thing. I beg the universe for patience. *Breathe in through the nose, out through the mouth...*

And then she asks the question I've been dreading: "So, your dad and I were wondering, what is your book about?"

I groan into my hands as my head thumps down onto my desk. My mother ignores my obvious discomfort and chatters. "Is it one of those murder mystery novels? I was just telling Donna Standish you have *such* a flare for drama, and that of *course* she could have a signed copy of your paperback."

One thought—and one thought only—flashes through my mind as my parents ramble on like I'm not even in the room.

I am going to *kill* Collin Keller.

If I don't kiss him first.

Tabitha: *So in the end, Mom and Dad were really supportive...*

Calvin: *I can't believe for a second you thought they wouldn't be.*

Tabitha: *I know, but you have to understand, I was really embarrassed.*

Calvin: *Why? It's not like any of us are going to read it.*

Tabitha: *YOU JERK! Greyson's gonna read it. COLLIN read it!*

Calvin: *But Collin only read it because he has a boner for you. That's totally different. No dude reads a romance novel unless he really likes a girl. Or wants to bang her. Just saying.*

Tabitha: *You're revolting.*

Greyson: *He's right about one thing, Tab. Collin genuinely likes you. Would you please put my brother out of his misery and call him. Or text him? He feels terrible.*

Tabitha: *God, I love these Group Chats [heavy on the sarcasm]*

Greyson: *Do what you want, but keep this in mind— it was an honest mistake. He cares about you, so much. He's a great guy, Tabby. Don't let your PRIDE get in the way of a great relationship.*

Calvin: *You and your damn Keller pride.*

Greyson: ^^^^ *Hey, smart-ass. I seem to remember you flipping out over a certain tweet before we started dating. You refused to talk to me for days #sexybeast*

Calvin: *Oh yeah, I totally forgot about that. Thanks for reminding me. Not.*

Greyson: *Aww, baby, but that's when I fell in love with you.*

Calvin: *I can't wait until tomorrow when I get to kiss those sexy lips of yours.*

Greyson: *YOUR lips are sexy. Rawr*
Calvin: *I love you*
Greyson: *I love YOU*
Tabitha: *HELLO! GROUP CHAT! Stop. Do NOT start sexting. OMG. How the hell do I take myself out of here? SOMEONE HELP ME. bangs on glass*

Collin

I've been waiting close to two hours at a table in the far corner, waiting to see if she'll walk through that front door. Tuesday and Wednesday she was a no-show, and yesterday I arrived a second too late, only to catch the taillights of her car pulling away.

But still, I wait.

Like clockwork for the past four days, hoping luck will be on my side.

The lukewarm mug on my table stopped steaming over an hour ago, the soy congealing at the bottom. I stir it to keep my hands occupied, but don't take a sip.

As fidgety and anxious as a crack whore, I tap the spoon on the saucer until a young woman at a nearby table brings a finger to her lips to shush me, shooting me a dirty look in the process.

Noted.

My legs bounces beneath the table restlessly.

Dammit, where is she?

Digging into the interior pocket of my jacket, I pull out the envelope tucked inside and smooth the wrinkles out with my palm, using the surface of the flat tabletop. I look up when the coffee shop door opens with a whoosh, a small cluster of leaves blowing in along with the brisk wind.

Holy shit, it's her.

She's here.

I fucking swear my heart skips a beat at the sight of her. It's only been a few days, but man, she's a sight for these hungry eyes.

I stand, moving towards her, and then double back because, shit, I forgot my envelope. It gets stuffed into the back pocket of my jeans before I call her name.

"Tabitha."

She places her bag at a table near a bank of windows and stills at the sound of my voice, her movements halted. Turning, just like in the movies—or a romance novel—her eyes widen at the sight of me. And she looks how I feel: tired. Weary. Desperate to stop the instant replay of what happened between us over and over in my mind and just wanting… something. Anything.

A resolution. A conversation.

Closure.

That's a damn lie; I don't want closure—I want her.

"Collin." Why doesn't she look surprised to see me?

"Hey," I say, approaching. My eyes drop to her laptop bag, and I cautiously let my lips curl into a tentative smile.

"What are you working on?"

She bites down on her lower lip, amused by the déjà vu. "Work stuff."

I can't get enough of this beautiful girl and her laidback sense of humor. Thank God she hasn't told me to fuck off.

Yet.

Relief sags my shoulders.

"What kind of work stuff?" I raise my hands and do air quotes, because I know she hates when people do that. I'm rewarded with a cheeky grin for my efforts.

Her hand goes to her hip. "What's with all the questions?"

"Just curious, that's all."

"Remember what happened the last time you were curious?" she asks, leaning against the large, overstuffed chair next to her table.

"Yeah. But I'm willing to take my chances." I pull the envelope out of my back pocket and extend it towards her. "This is for you. Could—would you read it? Please."

"Now?" She glances down at it, then at my face, studying it a few moments before reaching out to take the envelope. Our fingers meet when she does, and I'd like to think it was intentional on her part. Or maybe I'm delusional.

She shivers.

Nope. Not delusional.

My pulse quickens when she pulls out her chair and sits.

Awkwardly, I stand there, not sure…

"Would you sit down?" she demands. "You're making me nervous."

I sit, watching intently as she breaks the seal on the envelope, removes the thick cream paper from inside, unfolds it, and begins to read.

Tabitha

No man has ever written me a love letter before—not unless you count the time in seventh grade when Tim Bachman passed me a note in class describing how he wanted to feel my boobs. Did I want him touching me under my sweater after the soccer game? Yes or No. (Firm no on that one, by the way).

Unfolding a piece of cream stationary paper that looks like it's been read and refolded a few dozen times, my breath catches in my throat, because there in black ink and masculine script is a handwritten letter.

I bend my head and read.

Dear Tabitha,

I've never written a woman a letter before—not unless you count the time in eighth grade when I asked Melissa Spellman if she'd make out with me under the bleachers after the football game. She said no, by the way, so I guess we can't count that. So please, bear with me...

I don't know where to start, except to say that you're all I can think about, from the minute my eyes open in the morning—until I climb into bed at night. I would say I think about you when I close my eyes to sleep, but the truth is, I lie awake most nights staring up at the ceiling, trying to picture your face and remember the sound of your voice. Is that weird?

The other day When we argued and you walked out that door, it went against every one of my instincts not to chase you down. I panicked. I thought you were walking out of my life before our relationship had a real chance, and it scared the shit out of me. I can't say I'm sorry for what I said because you shouldn't have to hide how incredible. You know how I feel about you; I haven't played any head games and it kills me that people don't fucking know you've created something incredible. On your own, standing on your talent. Maybe to you it doesn't feel big. Maybe to you it doesn't feel remarkable.

But it is, holy shit, it is.

Is this the worst love letter you've ever received? Because that's what this is, so sorry about the swearing. It was hard for me to articulate how I feel—I don't have a way with words the way you obviously do. Numbers, yes. Words, no. I'm trying not to fuck this up. Is it working?

If you'll let me, I'll stand by and support you, whether you choose management for your parents' company or you want to write. I won't say another word about it.

I miss you. Let's start over.
Sincerely Love, Collin

I continue staring down at the letter, scanning it at least a dozen times, reading and rereading each word, over and over, devouring it, memorizing every line. Each and every beautiful, ineloquent word. Not because they're the most poetic words I've ever read, but because *he* wrote them.

He's the most fascinating man I've ever met.

He writes me sort-of love letters and works for a stock brokerage firm.

He's funny and smart and ridiculously good looking. He thinks I'm beautiful, smart, clever, and funny.

Collin believes in my dream.

Collin believes in… *me*.

And that's more than enough.

I bite down on my lower lip to stop the stupid grin spreading there, and raise my head, our gazes colliding. Tears moisten the corners of my eyes and I wipe them away, embarrassed.

"I'm sorry," I say, folding up the sheet of paper, lovingly tucking it into my laptop bag where it's safe and sound. Standing, I push back my chair and inch closer to where he stands regarding me.

I take a deep breath. "I overreacted—as usual—and I'm sorry. I might write romance novels, but the truth is, in reality… I'm complete shit at relationships."

His hand lovingly brushes some wispy stray tendrils of hair away from my jawline. "So am I."

"You're just saying that to make me feel better." I tilt my head into his palm, letting him cradle my cheek. "You've done nothing but try to win me over while I ran scared. For what? To push you away because I was lying to my entire family? This letter just proves what a fool I've been. Collin, this letter… it was…"

"*Don't* say sweet." He frames my face and plants a kiss on my nose before his hands glide down my ribcage to grip my hips, tugging me in, pulling our bodies flush. Mine gives a shuddering sigh.

It missed him, melts into him like a pile of magic sand. Like it belongs there.

"Fine, I won't." I lay my head on his chest, listening to his heartbeat, and wrap my arms around his waist with a whisper. "But it was. It was sweet *and* beautiful, Collin. The most beautiful thing anyone's ever written me."

"*You're* beautiful." His warm breath flirts with the shell of my ear. "I can't wait to get you home. I'll let you show me your gratitude then."

Oh, I just bet he does.

I wince. "Hey, Collin?"

"Yeah?"

"People are starting to stare."

"So? Let them."

So we do.

Taking Chances, a Novel by TE Thomas
Acknowledgements [re-edited]

This book means a lot to me, not only because it's my second novel but because along the journey, I think I might have found myself. But I didn't do it alone. I had the support of my family, my parents, my friends, and someone else.

To Collin: who discovered my writing all these months ago, before anyone else, and who believed in me when I didn't want to tell a soul about it. The past six months with you have been.... indescribable.

You love my writing, you love my wacky sense of humor, you love my pink "thinking" baseball cap. But most of all, I'm pretty sure you loved me at first sight. I can see it in your eyes when you look at me, and hear it in your voice when you whisper my name in the dark. You're my

best friend.
I love you, too.

Epilogue

Daphne

"Everyone raise your glasses in a toast," I announce around the high-top bar table, hoisting my wine glass in the air and encouraging Tabitha's friends to do the same. Clearing my throat, I begin. "We've gathered tonight to celebrate Tabitha, who's publishing her *second* romance novel." I put a hand to my mouth, pretending to whisper this next part. "Even though she kept it a secret from us in the beginning. Greyson, Samantha, Bridget—thank you for coming *all this way* to celebrate our friend! To Tabitha: we are so proud!"

"So proud!" Greyson echoes. "Seriously, Tab, Cal and I are so excited for you. Even though you used my *brother* as your muse for book two, which I cannot get past. Especially the chapter where you finally 'do it.' I will never be able to un-read that scene, and for that I will forever be ungrateful."

My best friend Tabitha, an author, laughs, her blue eyes sparkling with mischief. "Yeah, but the best ideas imitate real life."

I laugh, lowering my glass. "But do we have to *know* about it? Honestly. The visuals you gave us we could have lived without." Even though Collin is a complete hottie, and I don't mind for one second picturing him in the sack. Of course, I can't say that out loud.

I'm not *that* tacky.

Tabitha has the decency to blush. "I only used Collin to form the male character! I didn't use our *relationship* to plot the book!"

She can't even look us in the eye when she says it, the liar.

We all stare, our friend Samantha's expression clearly asking, *Who are you trying to kid right now*?

"You expect people to believe that? The whole second book is about two people who meet at a store; that's you. Then they bump into each other at a party. You. Then he finds out her secret. Also you. You, you, and you. *Your* story. Just admit it so we can finish toasting your success."

A dreamy smile crosses Tabitha's face. "Fine. I admit it. I was falling in love with him, so yes—I might not have done it on *purpose*, but it *is* our story."

"*Finally*. Now, as we were saying: here's to Tabitha, who we all knew would do something spectacular. Thank for proving us right. We love you and are so proud. Cheers!"

"Cheers to Tabby!"

"Hey," Bridget cuts in. "When do we get to *see* the famous love letter Collin wrote?"

Tabitha throws her head back good-naturedly, and face palms herself. "Oh crap. I forgot I put that in my book." She laughs the kind of laugh that makes a guy like Collin fall in love with you and write you love letters. "Sorry, ladies. The contents of said letter are private."

"Is it dirty?" Greyson wrinkles her nose. "Please say no."

"No! It's sweet. Ugh, the sweetest. Maybe someday I'll let you read it, but for now I'm enjoying keeping it to myself."

"Damn you and your secrets!" I complain. "I showed you the poem Kyle Hammond wrote me last year."

Half the table groans out loud, and Bridget smirks. "Are you *kidding* me right now? First of all, Kyle Hammond is a stalker that works in your office. Secondly, he plagiarized that poem off the internet. Third, it wasn't a love poem, it was a poem about a man's love affair with a married woman."

I scoff indignantly. "It's the thought that counts."

"He's just so adorable I can hardly stand it."

"Who, Kyle?"

"Collin," my best friend sighs in a daydream, resting her elbows on the bar table.

"Collin? Adorable?" Greyson laughs. "Okay, yeah—my brother is good looking. But I also remember him and his friends back in high school doing some pretty stupid crap, like toilet papering their friends' houses and leaving dead animals on the front porch that they found on the side of the road. Gross."

"What!" Samantha sputters, pausing with a wine glass

halfway to her lips. "Wait. *What*?"

Greyson nods with authority. "Yup, road kill. He and his football buddies would use it as their calling card when they'd go TP. Anything they found on the side of the road, they'd take and put on someone's porch."

"That's totally disgusting," Bridget adds, lifting her wine glass and pointing it in Tabitha's direction. "You kiss that mouth."

Greyson continues. "Skunks, opossums, squirrels, basically anything dead on the side of the road. Like, who *does* that?"

"I don't even know if I can drink any more of this." Bridget wrinkles her nose and stares down into her wine glass. "I think I just lost my appetite."

"Don't say you've lost your appetite, because I'm starving." Tabitha successfully changes the subject, her head swiveling around in search of a menu. "I think this place serves food. We should order something."

My stomach and I grumble at the same time. "It probably only serves bird food to go with this wine. Like cheese and dry fruit and crap."

"Whatever it is, we'll just order double."

Not seeing a menu, Tabitha hops down off her stool and dashes to the bar to fetch one, returning with a few and setting them in the middle of the table. "Have at it, ladies."

I crack one open. "Okay, this looks good: brie wedge and warm raspberry compote."

"Let's also do the artichoke dip and the bruschetta."

Bridget rubs her hands together gleefully. "Yes and yes. And look, they have crab cakes, but you only get three, so we'll have to order two."

"We're going to look like such slobs," I say, closing

the menu and signaling the bartender with the flick of a wrist in the air. "Is this table big enough for all this food?"

"Do you care?"

I shrug, the slouchy black satin shirt falling even farther down my shoulder. "Well, *no*…"

"Because I don't see any guys here about to sweep you off your single feet. We're free to do as we please."

"Must you point out the fact that I'm the *only* single one in this group tonight?"

"I'm sorry, that wasn't my point! I'm just saying…"

Bridget throws her hands up to stop our banter. "Hold that thought. Rewind! A group of guys just entered the building, three o'clock." We all crane our necks to get a good look, Bridget—the only one of us who's engaged—straining the hardest to catch a peek. "One of them is pretty hot."

"Um… what are you doing?" Greyson asks, grinning.

Bridget winks and tosses her long brown hair with a flip. "I'm scoping them out, of course. For *Daphne*."

The bartender walks over with her stylus poised above her tablet to take our order, and Greyson rattles off our selections, adding two more appetizers, along with another round of drinks.

"That should hold us over for a little bit," she says, handing back the menus. "Thanks." The bartender taps away on her tablet before nodding and walking off.

Bridget's eyes are glued across the room, her wine glass poised at her cherry-red lips. "What do you think those guys would say if they saw a shit ton of food show up at this tiny table?"

"What guys? Those guys?" Greyson's hazel eyes widen with surprise, and she cranes her head to look around the dimly lit club. "Why are you staring over there so hard? You're *engaged*."

If anyone should be ogling that hard, it should be *me*.

"Jeez, don't everyone look!" Samantha demands. "Yes, the guys who walked in before. They're at the bar now and totally checking us out."

Surreptitiously, we covertly sneak glances through the dim lights, towards the front of the wine bar. Sure enough, on the far side of the room, seated along the rails, a small group of guys are in fact checking us out, doing nothing to conceal their interest.

One of them even points.

I do a quick count of the math: four of them. Five of us. Unfortunately for them, I'm the only single one in this group. Well, I suppose we could technically count Samantha as single because she broke up with her boyfriend just days ago; her status might be single, but emotionally she's in no place to be picking up guys at a bar, sophisticated clientele or not.

We figured dragging her out tonight and plying her with alcohol would take her mind off of Ben & Jerry.

"Crap, they look like they're going to come over." Greyson groans miserably; if there's one thing I've learned about Grey, it's that she might be outgoing and friendly, but despite her stunning beauty, she's modest, private, and hates getting hit on.

I, however, do not. And apparently neither does—

"Samantha keeps staring!" Bridget accuses with a scowl. "You're going to give them false hope if you don't knock it off."

"I wasn't staring!" She huffs. "Alright, so what if I was? There's no harm in window shopping."

While they argue back and forth, not gonna lie, my ardent green eyes wander, seeking out the group of young men seated at the bar. They're not a large group, but they're loud and boisterous, with several flights of wine lining the counter like shots.

In my age range.

Several of them gather up their stemless wine glasses, their course of action to head in our direction. I stand taller, assessing.

The leader is a few paces above the rest, his laser-like focus hell bent to reach us first, undoubtedly so he can control the situation, or have first pick. Or both. I know his type—cocky swagger, lopsided grin meant to be captivating, tight white tee, and straining muscles that can only be obtained with hour upon hour at the gym. If that weren't enough, a visible tattoo snakes up the side of his neck and disappears into his hairline. Arrogant grin with blaring white teeth.

Wow. This guy thinks he's the shit.

The other three, well—they trail along after him like afterthoughts. The 'yes' men, donning the official uniform of "Mr. One-Night Stand": tight shirts, bleached teeth, and matching shit-eating grins. I bet two out of three of them have rib tats.

Except the straggler.

I eyeball the guy shuffling behind them, my green gaze *fixating* on him, latching on with fascination. Not only is he deliberately lagging behind, but he looks damn uncomfortable. This one… he's a complete paradox.

Dark, tousled hair, The Straggler effortlessly dons a gingham plaid shirt, neatly tucked under a preppy blue sweater vest and a belted pair of navy khakis. His only concession to casual: rolled shirtsleeves pushed to his elbows.

All he's missing is a bow tie.

Honestly? The poor guy looks like he's just arrived from the office—a tax attorney's office, I speculate. Or a cubicle at a technology company. Yeah, definitely computer programming.

Or insurance sales.

Wait, no. The Internal Revenue Service.

I bet he's an auditor; that sounds boring.

I'm not trying to be mean, but the guy is wearing *khakis* and a sweater vest in a bar on a *weekend*, for heaven's sake. He's practically begging me to judge him.

To the upwardly mobile, wearing a plaid shirt to a bar during the workweek would be just fine, but not on a Saturday. Unless, of course, he happens to be from the Deep South—maybe Georgia or South Carolina? Don't they wear bow ties down there? Yeah. They do.

I study him further and after some serious contemplation, conceding that The Straggler pulls off the stuffy look *just* fine.

And did I mention his glasses?

Kind of adorkable.

He pushes those tortoise-shell rims up the bridge of a straight nose on an average face, crosses his average arms across an average chest, and I watch as he tips his head towards the ceiling and murmurs to himself.

Adam's apple bobbing, I read his lips: *I'm in hell.*

Nope. I'm not eyeballing the guy because I'm interested; I'm eyeballing him because he's so *obviously* miserable.

Is it sick that I'm enjoying his discomfort? Ugh, what

is wrong with me?

Smirking, I bring the bowl of my wine glass to my lips, concealing the smile growing there as the guys approach, confidently, like a pack of vultures. Swallowing a chuckle, I gulp my wine.

"Hey, I think I recognize that guy," Tabitha says, her eyes squinting at The Straggler, then snapping her fingers. "*Ha*! Yes, I do. I'm pretty sure that's Collin's friend Dex. Dexter, I think."

Dexter.

I turn the name around inside my head, testing it out.

How nerdy.

But it fits.

And I like it…

Acknowledgements

Interesting fact: I didn't have acknowledgements for my first two books. Actually, I didn't have dedications either... Something else I didn't have? A clue.

Surprise, surprise.

Call me naïve, but when I started writing I had no idea what I was doing. I wrote for fun. I wrote what I wanted to read—and completely forgot to thank the friends in my life who helped guide me, and give me support I needed to make the novels a reality. Looking back on it, man do I feel crappy about it. (By the way, to this day, my Mom *still* brings it up.)

I've grown as a writer, and a human being, as so many new people have come into my life since my first novel published. So I want to start by thanking the people who have been with me along the journey.

Deep breath. Exhale.

Here we go...

I'm going to start with my Beta readers, who are my usual suspects: Kirstin Huie and Abby Slaven. Two incredible friends who have been with me from the beginning. Not only are they unbelievably supportive, they're also incredible young woman who inspire me daily. *Truly* outstanding individuals.

Nikki Kroll. I'm so glad you accepted my invitation to Beta. Your notes were spot on, perceptive, and useful. I look forward to the day I get to meet your beautiful face in person!

Tami Estes. I can't sum up how *fantastic* I think you are, and am grateful for all the suggestions you gave me on this book. Even though a "little bird" told me you were nervous to be honest with me, I am so thankful you were.

M.E. Carter: friend, writer partner, and pain in my ass. Not a day goes by that we don't bicker, banter—and give each other valuable insight. Sometimes you make me laugh, sometimes you make my face turn bright red (interpret that however you want), and sometimes... I wonder how the hell I ever existed without you. Someone was watching out for us the day our destinies collided.

Speaking of Destines Colliding... Shirl Rickman. Sweet. Funny. Enthusiastic. You're such a fantastic human being. Meeting you in person was one of the most exciting days I've experienced as a writer, and I want to forever be your road tripping partner. Road tripping, yes. Hiking, no. I (heart) you so much.

Laurie Darter and Dawn Chiletz—without your input, this book wouldn't have a plot. Honestly. I truly needed that brainstorming session at the Cheesecake Factory to pull me out of my slump. Not to mention, you're both so funny, caring, and... awesome.

Murphy Hopkins... what can I say about *you*? You are one kick-ass young woman. Creative. Witty. Passionate. Remarkable... these words feel a paltry description to sum up your character. Good days or bad, there is nothing you cannot do. Believe me when I say this: you inspire. We admire you.

Oh. And thanks for editing this book despite the fact that I forgot to book you.

Julie Titus (JT Formatting). Ugh, Julie, whom I've been dying to have format my books, and who has been incredibly patient with my pushing back dates—not once, but twice. Patience is your virtue, and I thank you. May we have a long, happy relationship...

To my dear friend Jen Cashin, who delights me with every selfie. Nothing makes me laugh more than pictures of you reading my books. It truly flatters me that you are so proud and supportive of me. I love you so much.

Vanessa Taylir for putting me in your library. That was the coolest day, and one of my proudest moments. You probably don't realize that, but... I can't tell you how much I appreciated your sending me the photo of my books in my hometown library. Best. Day. Ever. Love you.

Brenda. Katy. *Every* single day I think of you.

My sister Maddie, who needs a love story of her own. Now, if only she'd start listening to my advice...

Last, but not least – Christine Kuttnauer. You are the rock to my paper. One of the first people I speak to in the morning, and the last person I message at night—when we should both be sleeping, but are reading. Intelligent, *funny*. I love everything about you, including your flaws. You're you. And this book wouldn't have been written without you.

To my readers…. There is nothing—*nothing*—that fills me with more joy that seeing your positive responses to something I've written; I can't even describe what it feels like. Or what it feels like when someone simply writes on my Facebook wall. The level of happy is immeasurable.

I cannot wait to grow old with you all. Wait. That came out wrong… but you know what I meant.

I love you all.

For more information about Sara Ney and her books, visit:

Facebook
www.facebook.com/saraneyauthor

Twitter
twitter.com/saraney

Goodreads
www.goodreads.com/author/show/9884194.Sara_H_Ney

Website
http://kissingincars.weebly.com

Other Titles by Sara

The Kiss and Make Up Series

Kissing in Cars
He Kissed Me First
A Kiss Like This

#ThreeLittleLies Series

Things Liars Say
Things Liars Hide

Made in the USA
Charleston, SC
21 November 2015